William Maxwell

THEY CAME LIKE SWALLOWS

William Maxwell was born in 1908, in Lincoln, Illinois. When he was fourteen his family moved to Chicago and he continued his education there and at the University of Illinois. After a year of graduate work at Harvard he went back to Urbana and taught freshman composition, and then turned to writing. He has published six novels, three collections of short fiction, an autobiographical memoir, a collection of literary essays and reviews, and a book for children. For forty years he was a fiction editor at *The New Yorker*. From 1969 to 1972 he was president of the National Institute of Arts and Letters. He has received the Brandeis Creative Arts Award Medal and, for *So Long, See You Tomorrow*, the American Book Award and the Howells Medal of the American Academy of Arts and Letters. He lives with his wife in New York City.

INTERNATIONAL

BOOKS BY William Maxwell

All the Days and Nights: The Collected Stories (1995)

Billie Dyer and Other Stories (1992)

The Outermost Dream (1989)

So Long, See You Tomorrow (1980)

Over by the River and Other Stories (1977)

Ancestors (1971)

The Old Man at the Railroad Crossing (1966)

The Château (1961)

Stories (1956)
(with Jean Stafford, John Cheever, and Daniel Fuchs)

Time Will Darken It (1948)

The Heavenly Tenants (1946)

The Folded Leaf (1945)

They Came Like Swallows (1937)

Bright Center of Heaven (1934)

THEY CAME LIKE
SWALLOWS

THEY CAME LIKE SWALLOWS

William Maxwell

VINTAGE INTERNATIONAL
Vintage Books
A Division of Random House, Inc.
New York

FIRST VINTAGE INTERNATIONAL EDITION, APRIL 1997

Library of Congress Cataloging-in-Publication Data
Maxwell, William, 1908–
They came like swallows / William Maxwell.—1st Vintage International ed.
p. cm.
ISBN 0-679-77257-X
1. Family—United States—Fiction. 2. Women—United States—Fiction.
I. Title.
[PS3525.A9464T44   1997]
813'.54   dc21   96-46880
CIP

Author photograph © Dorothy Alexander

Random House Web address: http://www.randomhouse.com/

Printed in the United States of America
10 9   8   7   6   5

They came like swallows and like swallows went,
And yet a woman's powerful character
Could keep a swallow to its first intent;
And half a dozen in formation there,
That seemed to whirl upon a compass-point,
Found certainty upon the dreaming air . . .

—W. B. YEATS

CONTENTS

Book One
WHOSE ANGEL CHILD
3

Book Two
ROBERT
63

Book Three
UPON A COMPASS-POINT
135

THEY CAME LIKE

SWALLOWS

Book One

WHOSE ANGEL CHILD

I

Bunny did not waken all at once. A sound (what, he did not know) struck the surface of his sleep and sank like a stone. His dream subsided, leaving him awake, stranded, on his bed. He turned helplessly and confronted the ceiling. A pipe had burst during the winter before, and now there was the outline of a yellow lake. The lake became a bird with a plumed head and straggling tail feathers, while Bunny was looking at it. When there were no further changes, his eyes wandered down by way of the blue-and-white wallpaper to the other bed, where Robert lay sleeping. They lingered for a moment upon Robert's parted lips, upon his face drained and empty with sleep.

It was raining.

Outside, branches of the linden rose and fell in the wind, rose and fell. And November leaves came down. Bunny turned over upon the small unyielding body of Araminta Culpepper. Because he was eight, and somewhat past the age when boys are supposed to play with dolls, Araminta hung from the bedpost by day—an Indian papoose with an unbreakable expression on her face. But at night she shared his bed with him. A dozen times he drew her to him lovingly in sleep. And if he woke too soon and it was still dark, she was there. He could put out his hand and touch her.

Before him—before Peter Morison who was called Bunny—was the whole of the second Sunday in November, 1918. He moved slightly in order that Araminta Culpepper might have room for her head on the pillow. If it had been a clear day, if the sky were blue and full of sunlight, he would have to go off to Sunday school and sing hymns and perhaps hear the same old story about Daniel who was put in the lions' den, or about Elisha, or about Elijah who went to Heaven in a chariot of fire. And what would become of his morning? As soon as he got home and spread the funny-paper out on the floor where he could look at it comfortably, some one would be sure to come along and exclaim over him: *For Heaven's sake, it's too nice a day to be in the house. Why don't you go outdoors and get some exercise?* And if he pretended that he was going to but didn't, they would come again in a little while. He would have to put on his cap and his woolly coat and mittens, whether he wanted to or not. He would be driven out of the house to roll disconsolately in a bed of leaves or to wander through the garden where nothing bloomed; where there were only sticks and crisp grass and the stalks of summer flowers.

But not now, Bunny said to himself, hearing the sound of water dripping, dropping from the roof. Not this morning. And somewhere in the front part of the house a door opened so that his mother's voice came up the stairs. A spring inside him, a coiled spring, was set free. He sat up and threw his covers to the foot of the bed. When he was washed and dressed he went downstairs. His mother was sitting at the breakfast table before the fire in the library.

"How do you do?" He threw his arms about her and planted a kiss somewhat wildly on her mouth. "How do you do and how do you do again?"

"I do very well, thank you."

She held him off in front of her to see whether he had washed thoroughly, and Bunny noticed with relief the crumbs at his father's place, the carelessly folded napkin.

"Did you have a good night? Is Robert up?"

Bunny shook his head.

"Stirring?"

"No."

"I thought that would happen."

While Bunny settled himself at the table she buttered a piece of toast for him. When she had finished she lifted the platter of bacon from the hearth.

"Robert stayed up until ten o'clock, trying to finish *The Boy Allies in Bulgaria.* I told him they wouldn't assassinate anybody without him, but he wanted to finish it just the same." She helped herself to another cup of coffee. "You know how he is."

Robert was thirteen and very trying. More so, it seemed to Bunny, than most people. He wouldn't go to bed and he wouldn't get up. He hated to bathe or be kissed or practice his music lesson. He left the light burning in the basement. He refused to eat oysters or squash. He wouldn't get up on cold mornings and close the window. He spread his soldiers all over the carpet in the living-room and when it came time to pick them up he was never there; he had gone off to help somebody dig a cave. And likely as not he would come home late for dinner, his clothes covered with mud, his knuckles skinned, his hair full of leaves and sticks, and a hole in his brand-new sweater.

There was no time (no time that Bunny could remember) when Robert had not made him cry at least once between morning and night. Robert hid Bunny's thrift stamps and his ball of lead foil. Or he danced through the house swinging Araminta Culpepper by the braids. Or he twisted Bunny's arm, or showed him a fine new trick, the point of which was that he got his thumbs bent out of shape. Or he might do no more than sit across the room saying *Creepy-creepy-creepy* . . . pointing his finger at Bunny and describing smaller and smaller circles until the tears would not stay back any longer.

Before this day was over, it too would be spoiled like all the others. But while Robert was still upstairs in bed there was nothing for Bunny to worry about, no reason on earth why he should not enjoy his breakfast.

"It's raining," he said, and helped himself to bacon.

"I see it is." His mother took the plate from him and put it back on the hearth to keep warm for Robert. "It's been raining since five o'clock."

Bunny looked out of the window hopefully.

"Hard?"

Sometimes when it rained heavily for a considerable time he was not expected to go outside even though it cleared up afterward. The ground was too wet, they said. He might catch his death.

"Hard, Mother?"

"Like this."

Bunny tried to persuade himself that it was a heavy rain, but there was too much wind and not enough water. All the whirling and criss-crossing, the beating against the window and sliding in sudden rivulets down the glass—there was very little to it. The wind rose higher and the rain turned itself about and about. Inside, the room became intensely still. There was no sound but the logs crackling and singing in the fireplace. And because the lights were on in the daytime, the walls seemed more substantial, the way they

did at night with curtains drawn across the windows
and the room closed in upon itself.

"Do you think——"

Bunny hesitated, fearing at the last moment to ex-
pose himself.

"Rain before seven——" His mother got up from
the table, having read his thought and answered it se-
verely:

Rain before seven
Clear by eleven.

The words she had left unspoken remained cru-
elly before his eyes even when he looked down at his
plate. With great concentration he began to eat his
cereal. It would have taken a very little thing at that
moment to spill his sorrow. Let the clock catch its
breath, let one log fall with a sudden shower of sparks
up the chimney, and he would have wept.

His mother sat down in the window seat and
hunted through her sewing-kit impatiently. Bunny
could hear her saying to herself that he was a grown
man, or nearly so. Eight last August and not yet able
to depend on his own strength, but coming to her
again and again to be reassured.

Another time, he promised; another time he
would try and not give in to weakness. If only she
would not be severe with him now. He could not bear
to have her that way. Not this morning. . . . Feeling
altogether sorry for himself, he began to imagine what
it would be like if she were not there. If his mother
were not there to protect him from whatever was un-
pleasant—from the weather and from Robert and from

his father—what would he do? Whatever would become of him in a world where there was neither warmth nor comfort nor love?

Rain washed against the window.

When his mother found the needle she had been looking for, she threaded it. Then she took up a square of white cloth. Her hand flew this way and that, over her sewing. Quite suddenly she spoke to him: "Bunny, come here."

He got down from his chair at once. But while he stood waiting before her and while she considered him with eyes that were perplexed and brown, the weight grew. The weight grew and became like a stone. He had to lift it each time that he took a breath.

"Whose angel child are you?"

By these words and by the wholly unexpected kiss that accompanied them he was made sound and strong. His eyes met hers safely. With wings beating above him and a great masculine noise of trumpets and drums he returned to his breakfast.

2

"What are you making? tea towels?"

Bunny noticed that his mother had a very curious way of shaking her head. Rather as if she were shaking away an idea that buzzed.

"They *do* look like tea towels."

The interest he took in her affairs was practically contemporary. If she were invited to a card party he wanted to know afterward who won the prize, and what they had to eat, and what the place cards were like. When she went to Peoria to shop he liked to be taken along so that he could pass judgment on her clothes, though it meant waiting for long periods of time outside the fitting-room. Nor did they always agree. About the paper in the dining-room, for instance. Bunny thought it quite nice the way it was. Especially the border, which was a hill with the same castle on it every three feet. And the same three knights riding up to each of the castles. Nevertheless, his mother had it done over in plain paper that gave him nothing to think about, and might far better, in his opinion, have been used for the kitchen, where it wouldn't so much matter.

"If they aren't tea towels, what are they?"

He waited impatiently while she bit off the thread and measured a new length from her spool.

"Diapers."

The word started a faint spinning of excitement within him. He went thoughtfully and sat down beside his mother in the window seat. From there he could see the side yard and the fence, the Koenigs' yard, and the side of the Koenigs' white house. The Koenigs were German but they couldn't help that, and they had a little girl whose name was Anna. In January Anna would be a year old. Mr. Koenig got up very early to help with the washing before he went to work. The washing-machine galumpty-lumped, galumpty-lumped, at five o'clock in the morning. By breakfast time there would be a string of white flags blowing in the autumn wind. They weren't flags, of course; they were diapers. And that was just it. People never made diapers unless somebody was going to have a baby.

Bunny listened. For a moment he was outside in the rain. He was wet and shining. His mind bent from the wind. He detached a wet leaf. But one did not speak of these things.

Always when he and his mother were alone, the library seemed intimate and familiar. They did not speak or even raise their eyes, except occasionally. Yet around and through what they were doing each of them was aware of the other's presence. If his mother was not there, if she was upstairs in her room or out in the kitchen explaining to Sophie about lunch, nothing was real to Bunny—or alive. The vermilion leaves and yellow leaves folding and unfolding upon the curtains depended utterly upon his mother. Without her they had no movement and no color.

Now, sitting in the window seat beside her, Bunny was equally dependent. All the lines and surfaces of the room bent toward his mother, so that when he looked at the pattern of the rug he saw it necessarily in relation to the toe of her shoe. And in a way he was more dependent upon her presence than the leaves or flowers. For it was the nature of his possessions that they could be what they actually were and also at certain times they could turn into knights and crusaders, or airplanes, or elephants in a proces-

sion. If his mother went downtown to cut bandages
for the Red Cross (so that when he came home from
school he was obliged to play by himself) he could
never be sure that the transformation would take
place. He might push his marbles around the devious
and abrupt pattern of an oriental rug for hours, and
they would never be anything but marbles. He put
his hand into the bag now and drew out a yellow agate
which became King Albert of Belgium.

A familiar *thump* brought him somewhat pain-
fully again into the world of the library. *Thump
thump thump*—all the way across the ceiling. Robert
was getting up.

"I've been thinking—"

Bunny looked down in time to see his mother's
hand spread over his and enclose it.

"—about the back room. I told Robert he could
have a bed in there, and some chairs, and fix it up the
way he likes. He's getting old enough now so that he
likes to be by himself."

Bunny nodded. Sometimes when he and his
mother were alone they discussed Robert in this way,
and what should be done about him.

"If we do that, of course, there won't be anybody
to stay with you."

He liked to have her bend down and brush the
top of his head lightly with her cheek. But he would
have preferred another time. Now it confused him.
He turned his eyes toward the window and the damp
trees, toward the rain-drenched ground. As soon as
the window was clear enough for him to see through,

a fresh gust drove against it from the other side and everything blurred. It was that way when his mother kissed him. This talk about moving Robert into the back room, where his Belgian city was, where he kept his magic lantern. What had that to do with diapers?

"You see—" His mother spread the white cloth over her knees, folded it, laid it with the others in a pile. "What we need is another person in the family. At least one other person."

"I think we're getting along quite well the way things are."

"Perhaps. But the room you're in. It's ever so much too——"

Her hand opened and lay still.

Some one to fill up his room. Like the Mr. Crumb that stayed at Miss Brew's, three houses down on the same side of the street.

"We're not going to take in roomers, are we?"

"No, not roomers, exactly. I wouldn't like that."

"I wouldn't either."

Mr. Crumb had such a large nose. It would be upsetting to wake and find him in Robert's bed early in the morning.

"What I had in mind was a small brother or a small sister—it wouldn't matter which, would it? So you wouldn't rattle around in there the way you do when you are all alone."

"No, I suppose not. But does that mean—"

His mother was not satisfied with just him. She wanted a little girl.

When she got up and went out to the kitchen, he did not follow her. Instead he sat absolutely still, watching the yellow leaves contract; watching the spider swing itself out upon the ceiling.

3

Although the library had been familiar at breakfast time, Bunny knew that it was now subject to change, to uncertainty. His father had come home again and would be home, said the big clock in the hall, for the day. . . . The little brass clock with clear glass sides emerged out of a general silence, asserting that it was not so; that Mr. Morison would go out again after dinner. . . . They argued then. The grandfather's clock made slow involved statements which the other replied to briefly. "Quarter of ten," said the grandfather's clock, untroubled by the irrelevance. "Ten till," said the little brass clock on the mantel. So long as that went on, Bunny could not be sure of anything.

His father had settled himself in his chair, with the Sunday paper. From time to time he solemnly turned the pages. When he read aloud he expected everybody to listen.

"*What is Spanish influenza? . . . Is it something new? . . . Does it come from Spain? . . . The disease now occurring in this country and called 'Spanish influenza' resembles a very contagious kind of 'cold'*" *accompanied by fever, pains in the head, eyes, back, or other parts of the body, and a feeling of severe sickness. In most of the cases the symptoms disappear after three or four days, the patient rapidly recovering. Some of the patients, however, develop pneumonia, or inflammation of the ear, or meningitis, and many of these complicated cases die. Whether this so-called 'Spanish influenza' is identical with the epidemic of earlier years is not known. . . ."*

The word epidemic was new to Bunny. In his mind he saw it, unpleasantly shaped and rather like a bed pan.

". . . Although the present epidemic is called 'Spanish influenza,' there is no reason to believe that it originated in Spain. Some writers who have studied the question believe that the epidemic came from the Orient and they call attention to the fact that the Germans mention the disease as occurring along the eastern front in the summer and fall of 1917."

By the calm way that his father crossed one knee over the other it was clear that he was concerned with the epidemic for the same reason he was interested in floods in China, what happened in Congress, and family history—because he chose to be concerned with such things.

When Bunny was very small he used to wake in the night sometimes with a parched throat and call for a drink of water. Then he would hear stumbling and lurching, and the sound of water running in the bathroom. The side of a glass struck his teeth. He drank thirstily and fell back into sleep. . . . Until one

night across the intervening darkness, from the room
directly across the hall, a voice said, *Oh, get it yourself!* For the first time in his life Bunny was made
aware of the fact that he had a father. And thoroughly
shocked, he did as he was told.

Ever since that time he had been trying to make
a place for his father within his own arranged existence—and always unsuccessfully. His father was not
the kind of man who could be fit into anybody's arrangement except his own. He was too big, for one
thing. His voice was too loud. He was too broad in
the shoulder, and he smelled of cigars. In the family
orchestra his father played the piano, Robert the snare
drum, Bunny the bass drum and cymbals. His father
started the music going with his arms, with his head.
And in no time at all the sound was tremendous—filling
the open center of the room, occupying the space in
corners and behind chairs.

". . . *In contrast to the outbursts of ordinary
coughs and colds, which usually occur in the cold
months, epidemics of influenza may occur at any sea-
son of the year, thus the present epidemic raged most
intensely in Europe in May, June, and July. More-
over, in the case of ordinary colds, the general symptoms (fever, pain, depression) are by no means so severe . . .*"

Bunny saw that his mother was threatened with
a sneeze. She closed her eyes resignedly and waited.

". . . *or as sudden in their outset as they are in influenza. Finally, ordinary colds do not spread through*

the community so rapidly or so extensively as does influenza. . . ."

Bunny turned to his father. How was it that his father did not know? that he could go on reading?

"Ordinarily the fever lasts from three to four days and the patient recovers. . . . As in other catching diseases, a person who has only a mild attack of the disease may give a very severe attack to others. . . ."

The sneeze came. His mother's composure was destroyed by it. She fumbled for her handkerchief.

". . . When death occurs it is usually the result of a complication."

"James——"

"Yes?"

"Do you mind reading about something else?"

"If it will make you any happier."

The largest and the smallest of Bunny's agates raced along a red strip in the pattern of the library rug. Maybe his mother would come around to his way of thinking—that it was neither wise nor necessary to take on a baby at this time. Later perhaps. . . . Remembering the wallpaper in the dining-room he felt sure that she would go ahead with her plans. From what he had observed (he went to call on the Koenigs occasionally when there was nothing better to do) it would mean a great deal of confusion.

"Bunny, I've lost my handkerchief. Get me another, like a good child, will you?"

Bunny nodded. They would have to buy dresses, knitted hoods, and soft woolly sweaters. . . . The

race would be over in two shakes. Then he would get
the handkerchief. He could always finish what he was
doing before he got up and went on an errand for his
mother. It was understood between them. The smallest agate was dropping behind.

"Son. . . ."

The folded paper lay across his father's knees.

"Did you hear what your mother said?"

"Yes, Dad."

It was a very little way to that wide green opening
in the pattern which was the goal, with a chance that
the smallest agate might . . .

"Then what are you waiting for?"

His father spoke quietly, but his voice and his
firmness were like two unreasonable hands laid upon
Bunny's shoulders. Bunny knew even while he re-
sisted them that it was of no use. They would propel
him straight up the front stairs.

"Nothing," he said, and got to his feet.

From the doorway he looked back. The library
had changed altogether. In the chimney the dark red
bricks had become separate and rough. There were
coarse perpendicular lines which he had not noticed
before. And the relation between the pattern of the
rug and the toe of his mother's shoe escaped him.

The little brass clock had struck ten already, and
now the grandfather's clock in the hall was getting
started. There was a great to-do. The grandfather's
clock stammered and cleared its throat like an old
person. Once it had begun, nothing could stop it.

Though the house fell down, it would go right on, heavily:

Bonng . . . bonng . . . bonng . . .

And each sound as it descended through the air was wreathed and festooned with smoke from his father's cigar.

"*Charlie Chaplin married. . . . The bride, a motion-picture actress. . . .*"

Bunny saw black clothes, a mustache and cane, feet widely turned. About the baby, he decided—it was just as well that his father had not been told.

4

From somewhere out of sight, beyond the passageway, came a soft *tput-tput-tput.* . . . Sadness descended upon Bunny, sadness and a heavy sense of change. There was only one thing in the world that made such a sound: his steamboat. Robert had filled the bathtub with water and was playing with his steamboat.

Bunny stood and looked in the door of the back room, which was to be Robert's. It was now empty except for his village. Before long, Robert would have it. Robert's clothes would hang from hooks in the closet. Robert's shoes would tumble over each other on the closet floor. *Possession's nine-tenths of the law,* Robert always said when Bunny wanted his steamboat and Robert did not care to give it up.

That was because Robert was five and a half years older than he was. If *he* said that, Robert paid no attention to him. He had to get things from Robert by bargaining, or by appealing to his mother. Only she had said, definitely, that Robert was to have this room. It was all decided, just as it was decided what Robert was going to be when he grew up—*a lawyer*, Robert said to people who asked him. Always that; never anything else. (Bunny was going to be an architect.) Nothing would do but that Robert must practice law, try cases before a jury, like Grandfather Blaney. And be presented with a gold-headed cane, inscribed *To Robert Morison from the grateful citizens of Logan, Illinois.*

Nothing on earth could prevent Robert from becoming a lawyer; and in the same way nothing could prevent him from taking possession of the back room. Bunny knew that when the time came he would have to find another place for his blackboard and his magic lantern. He would have to pick up his Belgian village piece by piece and rebuild it in some other part of the house where people would be stepping over it every little while and complaining. And his magic lantern? What would he ever do about that? There were no dark green shades anywhere but in this room. His clothes closet had no window and was pitch dark, but it was not big enough. And besides, where would he attach the cord?

The soft *tput-tput* came to an end and Robert began talking to himself arrogantly. Bunny listened for a moment and then went and looked around the corner into the bathroom. Robert was declaiming, and in order to see his face in the mirror over the wash-stand he had pulled down the toilet-cover and climbed up on it. There balancing, he continued:

> *"And if thou sayst I am not peer*
> *To any man in Scotland here . . ."*

His sleeves were wet to the elbow, both of them. There was a tear in his stocking, acquired since break-fast. And one leg hung down, stiffly. Robert's *affliction*, people said, when he was not there to hear them.

Years ago, when Bunny was no more than a baby, and such a thin baby that he had to be carried on a pillow—Robert was hurt. Bunny knew only what he had been told. How Robert hopped onto the back end of a buggy and was run over. And they had to take his leg off, five inches above the knee. That was why Irene went up to Chicago and came back with the beautiful soldiers, the cavalrymen, which Robert kept on top of the bookcase, out of reach.

Now Robert was rehearsing. When he was satis-fied with certain gestures he bared his teeth at his re-flection in the mirror and going back a little, began:

> *"And if thou sayst I am not peer*
> *To any man in Scotland here,*
> *Highland*
>   *or low-land,*

> *Far*
>   *or*
>   *near,*
> *Lord Angus, thou hast*
>   *LIED!*"

The effect was fearful, even from out in the hall.
Bunny withdrew quietly and went into his mother's
room to get the handkerchief. Then he took it down
to her and came up again, this time by the back stairs.

5

Sunday morning was an excellent time for invading a
city. It was almost noon before Bunny's imagination
flagged. But very suddenly the scene changed. Walls,
gates, roofs, broken parapets and towers were then laid
bare in simple actuality—two collapsible drinking-
cups, a ruler, a block of stone, cardboard, brown
paper, three pencils, and a notched wooden spool.
After that it was no longer possible to pretend that
his lead soldiers were shouting to one another and de-
fending a Belgian town.

In actual weariness Bunny got up and went out to
the back hall, where the clothes-hamper stood, where
his mother kept the ammonia-bottle and rags for cleaning. She would know some way for him to pass the interminable time between now and time for dinner.

. . . He felt his way down the gloomy, boxed-in stairs.

She was in the kitchen when he found her, at the table, with spoons laid out in rows and the silver polish open at her elbow. Bunny sat down without a word, and twisted his legs through the rungs of the high kitchen stool. The kitchen always seemed older than the rest of the house, although it was not. Older and more seasoned. Bunny could remember being here before he could remember anything else. The walls were dark with scrubbing, and the surfaces shone wherever there was metal or porcelain. Turnip tops flourished in bowls along the window sill.

The spoons his mother was polishing were plain for the most part. Not very interesting to do. But she looked through them until she found one with her name written on it—*Elizabeth*—and with roses and pineapples, and the sun going down behind the Kentucky State Capitol. As soon as Bunny took up a piece of rag and began to polish his mother's name, the sadness slipped away. Now that he was in the kitchen beside her, it was impossible to care very much whether Robert got the back room or whether he didn't.

Outside, the sky was growing lighter. The rain came down unevenly, in spurts. The kitchen curtains were turning brighter, fading, and turning bright again. Bunny looked up in time to see the pantry door open. It was Irene, tall and straight-shouldered, in a blue raincoat.

"Surprise!" she said.

He threw himself upon her.

"Nobody told me you were coming."

"Surprise, I said!"

She took hold of him by his arms, above the elbow, and began to turn. Round they went in the middle of the floor with the room tilting this way and that. Round they went. Round his mother went, and the cookstove, and Sophie in a pink apron, and the sink . . . faster . . . faster . . . the table . . . the stove . . . the sink . . . table . . . stove . . . sink streaking longer . . . upward and longer. . . .

After they stopped whirling, the kitchen went round and round for a while, all by itself. Always when Irene came for Sunday dinner it was that way. His mother alone was calm and unshaken. She got up from the table and went to meet Irene. They kissed haphazardly, in front of the stove.

Irene was his mother's sister, but she did not resemble his mother in the least. Irene's hair was much lighter than his mother's, and her eyes were a different color. His mother was dark. Her hair was almost black, and so were her eyebrows, and she was much heavier. They both talked about dieting all the time. *An ounce of prevention*, they said, and then ate hard, awful-tasting biscuits with their tea. (With Irene it was just talk; she didn't need to be any thinner, but when his mother went to buy clothes, the saleswoman said, "Something for the stylish stout?") And their hands felt entirely different and looked entirely different. From Irene's hands he drew excitement, and from his mother's the fact that she loved him. Irene and his mother were as different as the two faces of a coin

And yet they never seemed conscious of the difference. They loved being together. And the things they said to each other had little meaning, often, for other people. For instance, if Irene remarked *Butter's what I'm after*—they both grew hysterical. When he inquired what was so funny about that, they didn't explain.

"Have you enough to eat, Bess?"

Bunny looked toward his mother and was relieved when she nodded. It would be a great pity if Irene went right away.

"I mean *plenty*," Irene insisted. "Because there's no use in my staying if it isn't going to be worth while."

Then without waiting for an answer she went to take off her coat.

Bunny followed discreetly at her heels. The dining-room as they passed through seemed braced and ready for excitement. Although it was only a quarter after twelve, the little brass clock in the library started to strike. Irene did that to things. Most people's rubbers came off easily, but one of hers now sailed halfway across the floor. The other had to be rescued from under the hall-tree. And the moment she began pulling at her gloves there was a great burst of singing from above:

> "*O when I die*
> *Don't bury me at all,*
> *Just pickle my bones*
> *In alkyhol . . .*"

Bunny felt called upon to explain.

"It's only Robert," he said. "Upstairs, playing with my steamboat." Then by way of an afterthought, "Where's Agnes?"

"At her Grandmother Hiller's. She's there for the day."

It was not an unreasonable place for her to be, though as a rule Irene and little Agnes came together. After dinner he and Agnes played house behind the sofa. Agnes was the mother. She made beds and dusted and swept and talked to the groceryman over the telephone (he was the grocery man) and had lunch ready for her fat sofa-pillow children when they got home from school. At the end of the day the father came home (he was the father) and spanked all the sofa-pillows that hadn't minded their mother and gave French harps to all that had.

Friday was the usual day for Agnes to go to her grandmother's. On Friday his mother and Irene went to their bridge club. After school he and Agnes walked home together—Agnes to her Grandmother Hiller's and he to his Grandmother Morison's, who lived with Aunt Clara and Uncle Wilfred Paisley in a square white house in the same block. At five-thirty his mother called for him in the car. Irene was with her and they were wearing their best clothes. And then they stopped and got Agnes. That was the way it usually was, and he wouldn't have thought anything about Agnes's being there today except for the fact that a moment ago Irene was bright and cheerful. Now she was staring moodily past the top of his head.

"Irene?"

Apparently she did not hear him. If he asked her what he wanted to ask her, she might not like it. She might call him a *curiosity cat*. To keep himself from asking, he watched her pocketbook swinging back and forth on the tip of her index finger.

"Irene, why is it that Agnes is at her Grandmother Hiller's?"

"She's there to see her father."

The pocketbook stopped swinging and slid to the floor. Bunny was deeply startled. He bent over and picked it up for her, but she did not seem to want it particularly. Agnes's father was Uncle Boyd Hiller, but he was not mentioned in the family. Or if he was, it was always by his initials—*B.H.* Never by his name. Not since the time they had to go to court to get little Agnes away from him. After that he went away and they didn't know where he was, or anything about him. Not for a long while. If he had come back now, it might mean all sorts of things. It might mean that he had come to take Agnes away. Or that Irene would have to go and live with him, the way she did before. It might mean——

The singing broke out again, on the landing, directly above them.

> " *'Tis better by far*
> *Not to spit at all*
> *Than to spit too far*
> *And hit the wall.*"

Robert appeared, steamboat in hand, singing. He
had made a half-hearted attempt at combing his hair,
but blond wisps stuck out in all directions. Irene's face
brightened as soon as she saw him. Robert, from the
very beginning, had been her favorite. But Bunny did
not mind. He had his mother. And besides, Irene never
thought he ought to be outdoors when he wasn't.

"Don't tell everything you know, Bunny."

Irene got up now and went toward the stairs.
Bunny shook his head. He did, sometimes. He did tell
everything he knew. But he didn't mean to. And this
time he was practically certain that Robert (who
didn't like to be kissed) would dodge suddenly before
Irene could catch him.

6

Irene had a way of making things memorable.

So it seemed to Bunny as his father held out his
mother's chair for her and they all sat down to dinner.

Because Irene was here, it was an occasion. Like
Thanksgiving or Christmas. They unfolded their napkins with a more than ordinary anticipation. What
they said was of no importance; merely to pass the
time until Sophie appeared with the roast chicken and
the occasion was confirmed. Then there were excla-
mations. His mother leaned forward anxiously, lest
the chicken fail to be as tender as it looked. Bunny

eyed the drumsticks. One of them went to him, as a rule.

"Hopefully yours," his father said, pointing the carving fork at him. And they all laughed. Even Sophie.

Then his father considered the chicken carefully. There was a moment of tension, and the knife slid in. Bunny could not help feeling that they would remember this afterward as the best roast chicken that ever they had.

"Just give me a little, James," his mother said—for she was always served first. "And no potato."

"Well you have to eat *some*thing. You'll get sick!"

"Yes, I know. . . . At the Friday club Amelia Shepherd was telling about a woman in Peoria who. . . ."

"There's no sense to it," his father said, gloomily. Then his disapproval passed, for lack of opposition, and he went on carving. A small slice of breast went to his mother, a much larger slice to Irene. When Robert got his wing, Bunny felt that he could look no more. He turned his head quickly and focused his attention upon the Japanese pilgrims who were climbing in and out among the folds of the curtains. He heard Sophie pass behind him and go back to the other side of the table. When he opened his eyes the drumstick was there, right on his plate. And the wishbone beside it.

Happily, Bunny looked about him at the circle of faces. His mother's eyes were dark brown, like his

own. Robert's were hazel. Aunt Eth lived in Rockford and she had hazel eyes also. But Irene's eyes were
gray.

Looking at her, he was reminded of his own
drooping shoulders (hers were so straight) and thrust
them back. No one noticed or thought to comment on
his posture, so he relaxed after a second and began to
eat.

The conversation became serious. There was talk
about the war, and how the rumor started that the war
was over. And talk about the last election, which his
father took into his own hands immediately. When
Bunny grew up he was going to vote Republican because his father was a Republican, and his father before him. It was all settled that way. Arthur Cook's father was a Democrat and they had a picture of President Wilson framed over the fireplace in their library.
But his father said that was all Tomfoolishness. When
Hughes was running against Wilson, Arthur Cook
wore a little brass mule on the lapel of his overcoat
and Bunny wore an elephant. And there was a time
when they didn't walk home from school together in
the afternoon. But that was all over now.

"Smart, I grant you——"

His father poured out the last spoonful of gravy
and gave the bowl to Sophie, to be refilled.

"Exceedingly smart. But he made the blunder of
a lifetime when he asked in the name of the American
flag that the people of this country re-elect a Democratic Congress. In the name of the flag he asked the
people for party control. And when he said that, he

stepped down from the high office of the Presidency and became nothing more nor less than the leader of the Democratic party. If there's any greater mistake that a President could make, I'd like to know it!"

Although his father looked straight at him Bunny knew that he was not supposed to answer.

The statement hung on the air unanswered, burning with force, with enormous conviction, while his father helped himself to mashed potatoes.

"And what does it get him? Just tell me that. He loses control of the House and the Senate, both. He's still President, of course. They can't take that away from him. And so long as this country is at war, people should support him along patriotic lines. But there's nothing in the Constitution which gives the President right to undivided control of the legislative bodies, in wartime or any other time. And when it comes to furthering his own personal ambitions and the ambitions of a group of Southern Democrats who completely upset the machinery of national expenditure and taxation—when you come right down to it—*risk* the economic welfare of this country in the interests of . . ."

Bunny twisted in his chair uncomfortably. He remembered something that he had meant to tell his mother. About Arthur Cook. When his father held forth in this way, the quiet which belonged to the dining-room seemed to have escaped to other parts of the house. He thought of the upstairs bedrooms and how still they must be. His mother was eating her salad quite calmly, in spite of President Wilson. When

she put her fork down, he might lean toward her and
—but it was not easy to describe things. Especially
things that had happened. For him, to think of things
was to see them—schoolyard, bare trees, gravel and
walks, furnace-rooms, the eaves along the south end of
the building. Where among so many things should be
begin?

Robert would not have had any trouble. *We
were playing three-deep*, Robert would have said.
And Arthur Cook got sick. That would have been the
end of it, so far as Robert was concerned. He would
not have felt obliged to explain how Arthur ran twice
around the circle without tagging anybody. And how
he stopped playing and said *I feel funny*. How he
went over by the bicycle racks then, and sat down.

"At school last Friday——"

But he had spoken too loud.

"How would it be, son——"

His father let President Wilson alone for a minute and turned his entire attention on Bunny, so that
he felt naked and ashamed, as if he were under a glar-
ing light.

"—if you kept quiet until I finish what I'm saying?"

That was all. His father had not spoken unkindly.
He was not sent from the table. No punishment was
threatened. Nevertheless, Bunny withdrew sadly into
his plate. And not even a second helping all the way
round could restore his pleasure in this day.

His father commenced eating, and the conversa-

tion broke apart. Robert began to explain about the
tie-rack he was making at school.

"You take and take a piece of wood about so
long——" He indicated how long, with his hands.

Bunny could tell at a glance that Irene was not
interested in Robert's tie-rack. He was not interested
in Robert's tie-rack, either. He was not interested in
anything of Robert's except the soldiers Robert would
not let him play with, which were Robert's dearest
possession.

"And when you get it planed down nice and
even, you take a piece of sandpaper . . ."

Through the dining-room window Bunny could
see Old John stretched out on the back porch with his
head resting on his black paws. John was very old and
decrepit. In winter he got rheumatism in his legs and
he had to be carried in and out of the house. Half his
days were spent in looking for bones that he had long
since dug up. And often he thumped his tail fondly
when there was nobody there.

Robert finished with the tie-rack eventually. And
then his mother and Irene exchanged recipes.

"I stir it," his mother said, "without ever chang-
ing the direction of the spoon. . . ."

"In cold water," Irene said, "and then I let it come
to a boil, slowly. . . ."

Once when they were in the bathroom and Irene
was in her thin nightgown, she said, *Bunny Morison,
stop looking at my legs!* And he could not stop blush-
ing. But why did she . . . And another time they

went for a walk out past the edge of the town. They carried a book to read, and sandwiches in a pasteboard box. At the first shady lane (it was in June) they turned off and settled themselves under a tree. Irene read to him out of the book, which was about boy heroes of Belgium. And a cow came on the other side of the fence and looked at them. When they got hungry they opened the box and ate all the sandwiches. That was over a year ago, and there was dust on the road. The air was heavy. Irene's voice sounded like swords clashing, slashing at the leaves overhead.

He tried now to get her attention, to ask her if she remembered that day when they went out beyond the edge of town, but her face was shadowed by inattention. By the same vacant look that she had a little while ago in the front hall. His mother was talking about Karl: Would his father arrange to have Karl come some day next week—Monday or Tuesday—and take down the screens?

Meanwhile, Robert, unhindered, had eaten a third helping of everything. He was buttering a slice of bread whole, which he shouldn't; he should break the bread into pieces and then butter it. And there would be very little left for Old John.

When Sophie came to clear the plates away, Bunny noticed that everyone at the table fell into a silence which lasted, usually, while she brushed away the crumbs and until she brought the cream for coffee. Over the dessert his mother and Irene fell to discussing clothes. Something was gathered, his mother said, with a pleat in the back.

Bunny could not see what they found in such matters to interest them. He could have left the table when Robert did, or when his father rose and went into the library to take his Sunday-afternoon nap, but there was still something that Bunny had to say to his mother. He waited until there was a break in the conversation; until Irene began thumbing the pages of *Elite*, which she had brought with her to the table.

"At school, we were playing three-deep——"

"Broad bands of sealskin——"

Irene held up the magazine for his mother to see.

"—with a hobble skirt."

"It's too tight-waisted," his mother said. "I'm not in the market for anything that isn't cut along the lines of a circus tent."

Bunny peered across the table, hoping to see the picture of an elephant, but there wasn't any. Nothing but women's clothes: coats that were *gathered*, he supposed bitterly, and blouses.

"Mother——"

"You could wear that, Irene."

His mother had taken the magazine and was thumbing the pages wistfully.

"But so could you!"

"Don't be silly."

"Don't *you* be." Irene was excited. The very smallest spark was enough to set her off. "You could copy it easy as anything, Bess. And with the fullness where it is . . ."

Bunny thought of the schoolyard: gravel and

dirt, with hardly a shred of grass; bare trees; the bicycle racks; and Arthur Cook's sick eyes.

"Mother, listen to me!"

He spoke louder than before, and plucked at her sleeve.

By the way her hand closed over his, he knew that she had heard him. All the time. And that sooner or later she would pay attention to nobody but him. Only just now he must keep still. He must not interrupt until they had finished what they were saying.

7

Bunny's nap was nearing its conclusion. Without making a sound, without moving, his body detached itself from the sofa. He moved freely among certain of the planets—Mars, the pink one, and Saturn with its rings. His dream, worn thin, began to give way around him. There was a moment of intense buzzing while he drifted back to earth. . . . Then, abruptly, he was awake.

Irene and his mother were having an important conversation at the other end of the living-room. Their voices were low and even, and he could just distinguish one word from another.

"You sure it isn't the war?" his mother said.

"Why should it be that?"

Bunny wanted to look at them, but he did not

dare. Irene might notice him and stop talking. As a rule, people did, if they saw he was listening. They said *Little pitchers have big ears*. On the other hand, there were ways of keeping from being noticed. Playing under tables and behind chairs, very quietly. Or if it was night and he was away from home, getting extremely sleepy, so that they had to put him on a couch somewhere and cover him up. After a while if he kept his eyes closed and breathed regularly, they thought he was asleep. That way he found out all sorts of things.

"Well, because"—his mother spoke more distinctly now—"because his company is ordered to France and you may not ever see him again. It could be that, Irene, and nothing more than that."

"It could be, but I don't think it is . . . I wish you'd seen him, Bess. He looks much older."

"So do we all. I found three gray hairs yesterday."

Bunny's mind stirred lightly within his shell. Around one of innumerable corners he came upon a staircase that he remembered—not the one here, not this staircase at home. He looked down, cautiously, and saw Agnes kicking and squirming in her father's arms. Agnes was frightened. She kept saying, *I want my mamma . . . I want my mamma . . .* over and over. Whose house it was Bunny did not know. The remembrance was cloudy and uncertain, like a dream remembered in the midst of breakfast: Uncle Boyd carrying Agnes in his arms and the door closing upon them. There was meaning to it, and possibility of explanation; only he never dared to ask. And then Irene walked past him, talking to herself. He spoke to her, but she didn't even know that he was there. At the head of the stairs she waited, as if there was something she had just that minute thought of. Then she fell down, one step at a time, bumping.

"He looks older in a different way, and sad. It's very hard to explain, exactly."

"No doubt."

"But if you'd seen him! It's as if he were thinking all the time—even while he is making polite conversation—that he'd missed something people can't afford to miss."

"Whose fault could that be?"

Bunny had never heard his mother's voice sound quite so dry and unbelieving.

"His own, I suppose—but everything's that, in a way, for everybody."

"In a way. But I remember the last two months that you lived with him. I remember that you were like a crazy woman."

"I know I was. Though much of it was on account of Agnes. He was so jealous. But when I try to remember his fits of temper, and how unreasonable he was, I think of all sorts of things *I* started."

Through eyes that were nearly closed Bunny caught a glimpse of the living-room: moss-green wallpaper, and the green carpet, and a well of green shadow in the far corner of the room where Irene and his mother sat talking. He was not entirely awake, so that he saw things peculiarly. The white woodwork was unattached to the walls. The shape of the chairs was ambiguous. At a word from him (a magic word) the sofa would curve its back differently and the chair-arms protrude bunches of carved wooden grapes. The golden bowl which was suspended upside-down from the ceiling by three chains was now the size of a buckeye cup and now as large as the wading-pool at the Chautauqua grounds. Time and again, while he squinted his eyes, the walls relaxed and became shape-less.

He lost track of the conversation and when he started listening again, Irene was saying, ". . . and she had her son with her, a youngster about eleven years old. And every time they came on deck she'd light into him because he was sending all his post-cards to the same boy, instead of spreading them around.

"Boyd couldn't see anything funny in that, and after I explained, he still wasn't amused. It was com-pletely unimportant . . ."

Bunny's eyelashes brushed and became momen-tarily entangled. Against the light from the bay win-dow they seemed as large and long as spears. His mother got up and went over to the mantel. Then she came back and sat down again, with a box on her knee.

"Will you have some candy?"

"So soon after dinner. How can you, Bess?"

"You've forgotten what it's like to be—"

"Oh, of course. I did forget, as a matter of fact. I mean I forgot you were— But it is important that people laugh at the same things. Or at least enjoy them in something like the same way."

"If you went back to him, Irene, you'd find——"

"He was there when I took Agnes, this noon. I went in, anyway. I shouldn't have, I suppose. But I thought what's the use of going out of my way to make trouble when there's been enough already."

The last time Uncle Boyd came to the house, before he went away, Bunny saw him. Bunny was playing in the front hall with a china wolf-hound that used to be at Grandmother Blaney's before she died. And he looked out of the front window and saw Uncle Boyd coming up the walk. The doorbell rang. His father came to the door and opened it. And there he was —tall and thin, with a gray streak across his hair. And he said, *Is Irene here?* And his father said, *I haven't the least idea!*

"Boyd was very pleasant. He asked after you, Bess, and said how much he thought of you——"

"Yes?"

"And when I got up to go, he went with me as far as the front walk. We stood by the hitching-post and I said good-by, and he said good-by and he was very glad to have seen me, and then he shook hands very formally as if I were a visiting lady from Scotland. And then he went all to pieces. . . . The things he said—you wouldn't believe me if I told you. Standing there on the sidewalk with the tears running down his cheeks. . . . It was a mistake. For two whole years he had known it was all a mistake. And the way he found out was that he caught himself looking for me wherever he went. He'd notice some woman at the theater or walking in a park, and the back of her head would be like me. And he'd follow her, thinking possibly . . ."

Bunny narrowed his eyes as his mother got up, with the box of candy in her hand, and put it on the mantelpiece, where it wouldn't be so continual a temptation. Then she said, "Speaking of the backs of women's heads—I took Robert aside the other day and made him promise that if anything happened to me he'd break all my cut-glass. I don't want some other woman using it when I'm gone."

Bunny's eyes flew open. In the nick of time he remembered that he was pretending to be asleep, closed them, and opened them again—more deliberately. The spears waved. He was in a field of green corn.

8

The intense part of the afternoon was over when Irene got up to go home. Bunny and his mother were alone after she left. And it was clear that his mother was despondent over something, for she stopped hemming diapers and gazed thoughtfully into the fire for a long while. Once she sighed.

At the right moment Bunny told her about Arthur Cook, and how Arthur got sick at school. Bunny heard the nurse telling his teacher, outside in the hall, that it was a clear case of flu. This time there was no doubt about his mother's interest. She sat looking at him anxiously, the whole time. And certain portions of his narrative had to be repeated.

"Bunny, why didn't you tell me? Why didn't you tell me last Friday, instead of waiting until now?"

He started to explain fully, but she had already picked up the receiver of the telephone.

"I'm going to call Arthur's mother, and find out how he is. And while I think of it, there's something you can do for me: We're out of cream. Sophie forgot to order any. And if I make cornbread for supper, we'll need butter as well. Half a pound. . . . *Nine-nine-two*. . . . *Yes, that's right*. . . . I could send Robert for it when he gets home from Scout meeting, but he may be late."

It was the unexpected that happened, always. The empty gun, his Grandmother Morison said, that killed people. He would have to put on his rubbers and his coat and cap and gloves and go outdoors.

Weekdays he came straight home from school so that he could have his mother all to himself. At quarter after four Sophie wheeled in the teacart and there was a party: little cakes with white icing on them, a glass of milk for him and tea for his mother. Then he sat on her lap while she read to him from *Toinette's Philip* or from *The Hollow Tree and Deep Woods Book*. About Mr. Crow and the C-X pie. Or about Mr. Possum's Uncle Silas who went to visit Cousin Glenwood in the city and came home with a "man" and a lot of new clothes and a bag of shinny sticks.

When his mother read to him, her voice fell softly from above. It turned with the flames. Like the flames, it was full of shadows. While she was reading he would look up sometimes and discover that she had yawned; or she would stop and look into the fireplace absently, so that he would have to remind her to go on reading.

But today there was no pleasant hour with her before his father came home. When he threw open the back door, the sky overhead was clear, the air thin and without warmth. Old John rose and extended his paws unsteadily. Bunny recognized it as a gesture toward following him. But having made the gesture, Old John could do no more. He collapsed feebly upon his square of carpet.

If it had been Robert, Bunny thought sadly—if it had been Robert that called him, Old John would have come along.

Hoping to catch something off guard, he crossed the garden walk. But the sunlight was spread too evenly upon the ground and woven too firmly into the silence under the grape-arbor. Bunny did not disturb it in the least by his coming. Only the Lombardy poplars were a trifle unprepared, so that when he picked up a stick and broke it, their few remaining leaves were seized with a musical agitation.

For a second Bunny wanted to climb up on the kitchen roof, which started behind the flue and from there sloped down almost to the ground, over the cellar stairs. Then he turned and went directly toward the front walk. An iron picket was missing from the fence. Once upon a time he could slip through by ducking his head. Now he had to bend double and squeeze. He was growing. Size nine or nine and a half. And yet the sidewalk seemed no farther away than it had ever been. With his head down, his eyes fastened upon the cement, he started toward the store.

> *Step on a crack*
> *You'll break your mother's back*

At the corner he looked up, for no reason. The outer branches of the elm trees met high overhead, shielding the street, which was empty and strewn with dead leaves. Mrs. Lolly's store was in the next block. Her porch was old and rickety and sagged in places, but it was high enough to stand up under. On the hard ground underneath Mrs. Lolly's porch three boys were kneeling, their arms outstretched, playing marbles. Johnny Dean, Ferris (who smoked cigarettes), and Mike Holtz. The afternoon became complicated—though it was clear, after the rain, and transparent to the farthest edges.

At the intersection Bunny crossed over. His knees were becoming drowsy with fear. He could go back, of course. He could go home and come again a little later. But what would his mother think? Opposite the store he crossed back again. Mike Holtz didn't see him, but he saw Mike Holtz. Saw his white face, jeering, his cap pulled down over one ear, his dirty fat knuckles. . . . If he could get as far as the steps, Bunny told himself carefully. He came to the steps, mounted over the very center of his fright, and closed the door safely behind him.

Mrs. Lolly was middle-aged and sagging, like her porch. She kept a yellow pencil in the knot at the back of her hair. Bunny was grateful to her, as he was grateful now to all things—things standing about in boxes and cases, on shelves all the way up to the ceiling. Everything was so substantial. The crates of apples and oranges, the pears in tissue-paper, the enormous cabbages. And most substantial of all—a very old woman who was worrying with her shawl.

Mrs. Lolly added up figures on a paper bag. When she stopped and looked at him blindly, Bunny saw that her eyes were full of arithmetic.

"Are you in a hurry?"

He shook his head. Not at all in a hurry. Not in the least. What he most wanted was for time to stand emphatically still, the way the sun and the moon did for Joshua.

The old woman, waiting, sucked at her teeth one after another until the pin came out of her shawl.

"Seven"—Mrs. Lolly went on counting—"and two to carry."

Bunny pressed his nose against the glass case. Looking intently, he tasted gumdrops, licorice, caramels, candy-corn.

"In Chicago," the old woman said, as she fastened her shawl closely about her shoulders, "I hear there's people dying of influenza. And in St. Louis."

A pleasant imaginary voice said: *Help yourself, Bunny. Take as much of anything there is in the case as you want.*

Mrs. Lolly jabbed the pencil straight into her

head. "There's lots of sickness about," she said. "Come in again." And with what was left of the same breath, "Young man?"

"Cream," Bunny told her. "And half a pound of butter."

Then hoping by one means or another to delay matters he went in pursuit of Mrs. Lolly's tortoise-shell cat.

The cat dived under a cracker-barrel.

"Anything else?"

Mrs. Lolly held the cream out to him, and butter from her ancient ice-box. With no reason to stay, and nothing left to ask for, Bunny turned away. He and the old woman went out together. The steps were wet and so they both went slowly. When the old woman reached the sidewalk she stopped to catch her breath and went *phifft*—with her finger against her nose. Disgust encircled Bunny's throat.

Crossing the street in the old woman's wake, he remembered the first time he had ever seen anyone do that. A farmer. Some one they drove out in the country to see about some insurance premiums. His father left the car at the farmhouse. They climbed under a fence and walked side by side through a meadow where daisies were growing. And they came to a field and the man was in the field with his horses. His father talked about the price of wheat—whether it was better to sell now or hold on to it awhile. And everywhere about them the green corn was making a sound like——

"*There* he goes!"

A voice sang out, with no warning. The voice of Fat Holtz. The trees stumbled and the sidewalk turned sickeningly under Bunny's feet. He ran, ran as hard as he could, until legs tripped him from behind and hands sent him sprawling in the bitter dirt.

How Robert came to be there, who summoned him in this hour of need, Bunny did not know. Robert was there. That was enough. Robert pulled his tormentors off, one by one, and drove them away. Bunny sat up, then, and saw that there was a large hole in his stocking. And his knee was bleeding.

"Before all my friends," Robert said.

Matthews and Scully and Berryhill and Northway were crossing over to the other side of the street. They did not look back.

"In front of everybody," Robert said; "and you didn't even try to hit them."

Robert, too, was against him. Bunny looked at the broken glass and the white stain spreading along the walk, and burst into tears.

9

The little brass clock on the mantel struck seven sharply, to make clear that this second Sunday in November, 1918, which had begun serene and immeasurable, was very nearly gone.

From his place in the window seat Bunny ob-

served that the rug was a river flowing between the
stable and the long white bookshelves; turning at the
chair where his mother sat, with light slanting down
about her head and the blue cloth of her dress deep-
ening into folds, into pockets.

When the little brass clock finished, the grandfather's clock cleared its throat, began to stammer. In
the midst of this mechanical excitement Robert took a
firmer hold on the lamp cord and with his free hand
turned a page of *Tarzan and the Jewels of Opar.*

When the grandfather's clock had finished, it was
seven (officially) and Bunny exchanged glances with
his mother. His father got up to put a fresh log on the
fire. Then he took a pack of cards and laid them face
down in rows on the library table. His father grew
restless if they remained overlong at the dinner table;
fidgeted; contrived ways of transferring the conversation bodily to the library, where he could begin his
shuffling and turning, his interminable dealing of
cards. Bunny turned back to his mother.

"For this time of year," she said, "for November,
it seems to be getting dark too soon."

She meant what she said, of course. And she
meant also whatever she wanted to mean. Bunny was
not surprised when his father stopped turning the
cards and looked at her.

"I hadn't noticed it."

In this fashion they communicated with each
other, out of knowledge and experience inaccessible
to Bunny. By nods and silences. By a tired curve of his
mother's mouth. By his father's measuring glance over

the top of his spectacles. Bunny drew his knees under him and looked out. The room was reflected in the windowpane. He could see nothing until he pulled the curtain behind his head. Outside it was quite dark, as his mother said. Light from the Koenigs' window fell across their walk, across the corner of their cistern. If he were in the garden now, with a flashlight, he could see insects crawling through the cold grass. If he waited out there, waited long enough, he would hear blackbirds, and wild geese flying in migratory procession across the sky. . . . The curtain slipped back into place. Once more he could see nothing but reflections of the room. The night outside (and all that was in it) was shut away from him like those marvelous circus animals in wagons from which the sides had not been removed.

"I stopped in to see Tom Macgregor this afternoon," his father said.

"Seven of diamonds, sweetheart."

"I *see* it."

"Now, maybe, but you didn't."

Although she never paid any attention, his mother seemed to know by instinct when his father turned up the five of spades or the seven of diamonds that he was looking for. And she could tell clear across the room when his father began cheating.

"I did, too."

"Jack of clubs, then. . . . How was he?"

"How was who?" his father asked.

"Tom Macgregor."

Bunny listened with quickening interest. It was

Dr. Macgregor who took his tonsils out; who sewed up a long gash over Robert's eye the time he fell off his bicycle, so there was scarcely the sign of a scar.

"He has a new hunting-dog."

"How many does that make?" His mother sat up suddenly and poked through her sewing-kit until she found the package of needles.

"Three, as I recall. But one of them has worms. I couldn't get him to talk about anything else."

"Did you see it, Dad?"

His father drew all the cards together and sorted those which were lying face up from those which were face down. Bunny could not bear, sometimes, having to wait so long for an answer.

"Dad, did you *see* the dog that had worms?"

"Yes, son."

"What did it look like?"

His father shuffled the deck loudly before he spoke.

"It was an English setter."

Bunny got up from the window seat in despair; he would go out to the kitchen and pay a visit to Sophie, whose conversation did not leave off where it ought to begin.

To get to the kitchen he must go through the dining-room, which was almost dark. And then the butler's pantry, which was entirely so. It was safe and bright in the kitchen, but overhead were dark caverns that Bunny did not like to think about—that end of the upstairs hall, where there was usually no light on, and the terrible back stairs.

"I think I'll go see what Sophie is doing."

His mother's nod reassured him. It said *Very well, my darling, but go quickly and don't look behind you.*

Under the pantry door there was a line of yellow light. And Bunny heard voices—Sophie, Karl, Sophie again. They were talking to each other in German, but they stopped when he pushed the door open. "Hello!" he said. The warm air of the kitchen enveloped him, instantly.

"And how is Bubi this evening?"

Karl was sitting very straight in the kitchen chair with his raincoat on. Tiny rivers of sweat ran down the sides of his face.

"My name isn't Booby, it's Bunny!"

"*Hein?*"

No matter how many times he corrected Karl, it was always the same. Karl never could remember. He always put his great hands together over his stomach and bobbed his head.

"That is good. And I all along was thinking—what you say it is? . . . *Bubi?*"

Sophie laughed then, and rattled the dishes in the kitchen sink—although there was no particular reason, so far as Bunny could make out, why she should do either. Every Sunday night this same conversation took place. Karl appeared after supper, scraped his feet on the mat, rain or shine, knocked once very gently, and came in. While Sophie washed and dried the dishes, Karl sat waiting with his coat on. And if Bunny came into the kitchen, Karl lit his pipe, gathered Bunny onto his lap, and told him a story.

After this unsteadying and unreasonable day when he had had so much to think about (the baby coming and Robert taking possession of the back room), after his encounter with Fat Holtz, Bunny gave himself up to the smell of leather and pipe tobacco; to the comfort of Karl's shoulder.

The story was always the same. Following the certain channel of Karl's sentences (*Already the ditch so deep was . . .*) He saw Karl's great-grandfather digging in mud and water up to his ankles. He saw trees falling, heard the great wind that blew and blew out of the ditch until at last it blew Karl's great-grandfather's pipe out—as Bunny was sure it would. And no sooner did Karl's great-grandfather's pipe go out than the real pipe which Karl held between his teeth, a deep-bowled one, went out also. And Karl had to stop and fill the real one before the story could go on.

First he couldn't remember what he had done with his tobacco-pouch. He looked earnestly on the kitchen table, under the chair, in all his pockets. He felt the sides of his trousers. He made Bunny get down so that he could search through his raincoat half a dozen times. After the pouch was located (in Karl's inside coat pocket, where he always kept it) Karl had to fill his pipe with great care. He had to tamp it down so that it was not too loose and so that it was not too tight. Then one match after another, before the pipe was lit properly. And just as Bunny was climbing back on Karl's lap, Sophie gave a final twist to her dishrag and hung it over the kitchen sink.

"*Aber* next time . . ." Karl said, smiling at him from the doorway.

But I wanted to hear the ending of the story now, not next time, Bunny thought sadly, as he turned out the light and made his way with one hand along the wall until he reached the dining-room.

"I told you, Bess. . . . There isn't any place else for her to go."

His father and mother were in the library still. By the tone of his father's voice Bunny was sure they were discussing Grandmother Morison. He waited for a moment among the dining-room chairs until he could decide whether the conversation was worth overhearing, and learned that Uncle Wilfred and Aunt Clara were going to spend Thanksgiving in Vandalia, with Uncle Wilfred's family.

"Why does your mother have to go any place? Why can't she stay right there while they are away? They could get some one to come in nights so that she wouldn't be alone."

"They're going to close the house up. The gas and electricity will be turned off."

"For *five* days?"

"Yes."

Bunny thought of Aunt Clara's house, standing there on the other side of town. And how Grandmother Morison and he went up the narrow stairs that lay behind a door in the Spare Room. Up to the attic which was Unknown Land, full of boxes he was not

encouraged to look into, pictures, vases, trunks, broken
pieces of furniture, magazines, books, old clothes—so
much of everything and so many things that he could
never get more than a confused geographical impres-
sion of the whole. By the double flue were toys that
had belonged to Cousin Morison when he was a little
boy. These he was not allowed to touch. . . . By
the second dormer window was another collection,
which belonged to Robert. Not so many, of course.
Few of Robert's toys survived the treatment he gave
them. Bunny was not allowed to touch these, either.
. . . In the far corner of the attic beside the water-
tank were his own toys, all carefully put away in an
egg-basket. These he could take down with him to
Grandmother Morison's room, which smelled of
camphor.

While she made quilting patterns out of brown
tissue-paper, he played with the lovely Russian sleigh
that worked on spools. With the paperweight Lion of
Lucerne. With tables and chairs for the house where
the three bears lived. And there were pictures in the
basket, as well as toys. Pictures of Daniel, of Ezekiel
in the valley, of Joshua with his sword drawn, bidding
the sun and the moon stand still.

Bunny could not help regretting those other toys
at Aunt Clara's which he was never allowed to play
with. Especially the little gold piano with angels
painted on it. Once, as he was going by, he put out his
hand and touched one of the keys. And Aunt Clara
called up to him through the floor that the little piano

was Cousin Morison's (who died of typhoid fever) and he was not to touch it.

"I'm telling you what Clara said."

Bunny moved closer to the doorway. If he went any farther they'd stop talking, but at his back was the dark pantry, and the door into the kitchen was wide open.

"If it were at any other time. But we'll both be gone, and you know there's no telling what she may take into her head to do. I don't really mind her straightening my dresser drawers—I do mind, as a matter of fact—but she feeds Bunny gumdrops and horehound candy until his stomach is upset, and tells Sophie she won't go to Heaven because she was baptized in the Lutheran Church. . . . And what about Irene? Shall I tell her that we've changed our minds and don't want her to stay with the boys while we're away?"

"No, I'd rather she were here."

"So would I. Much rather. But the house isn't big enough to hold Irene and your—"

Bunny's question was decided for him by a disturbance on the back stairs—so sudden that his terrified heart nearly stopped beating. With arms outstretched he threw himself bodily upon the lighted room.

10

While Bunny waited, the cymbal in his left hand and
the large padded drumstick in his right, Robert beside
him tapped delicately on the edge of his chair. Light
shone on the varnished surface of the piano, on the
ivory keys. His father's hands proceeded up the key-
board in a series of chords twice repeated. Across the
living-room his mother was looking at them. She was
waiting for them to begin.

"Well, gentlemen?"

Bunny met his mother's eyes at the precise moment when his father started forth upon the opening
measures of *Stars and Stripes Forever*. The flood of
sound was so sudden and so immense that Bunny came
near drowning in it. He caught at the regular six-eight
rhythm as if it were a spar, and striking out with the
cymbal in his left hand, the drumstick in his right, he
tried frantically to save himself.

> *Ching . . .*
> *Boom . . .*
> *Ching . . .*
> *Boom . . .*
> *Boom . . .*
> *Boom . . .*
> *Boomdiddy-boom-boom . . .*

Once started, the music swept along of its own momentum, carrying Bunny with it. He was helpless. So was Robert and so was his mother. The only opposition came from the room itself. What the green walls threw back, the fire caught at and sent up the chimney. What the fire could not reach, the ringed candelabrum turned nervously into light, ring upon ring.

After *Stars and Stripes Forever* came *Washington Post* and *El Capitan* and *The Fairest of the Fair*. Bunny's eyelids began to grow heavy. They were weighed down with music. He told himself anxiously that he must keep them open. He must not drop off to sleep. But in a very short while there was Karl's great-grandfather digging and digging with a pipe in his mouth . . .

digging . . .

and the water seeping into his ditch . . .

and the air grown darker . . .

and the high wind . . .

"Now what's wrong?"

The music had stopped and Bunny saw to his amazement that he was at home, in the living-room. And his father was frowning at him.

"He was falling asleep," Robert said.

"You can't expect to play with us, son, if you're going to fall asleep every five minutes. See if you can't do a little better."

Bunny stared self-consciously in front of him, past Robert's grave smirk.

His father turned back to the piano and with his

left hand struck a chord, then another. "We'll quit in a few minutes and then you can go to bed." They took up *The U. S. Field Artillery* where they had left off. Bunny forced his eyelids so wide apart that they ached. If his mother would only look at him! Through the fading light he saw that she was reading. She had picked up a magazine. His eyelids closed for a second and when he opened them the room had darkened permanently. There was nothing, he found, that he could do about it. He heard the rhythm of the piano. Cymbal chinked blindly on cymbal and drumstick beat drum. But he was wrapped comfortably around in music so deep and so firm that he could lie back upon it. He was upheld for a long time and then moved forward into a darkened air where thunder burst concentrically out of red rings . . . green rings . . . lavender rings . . .

"For the love of God!"

"I wasn't falling asleep!" Bunny said, so wide awake now that he thought he was telling the truth.

"Oh balls!"

What this word meant when it didn't mean a ball that you throw or bounce, Bunny had no idea, but he knew it wasn't nice, whatever it was. And imprisoned inside him was another little boy who was nobody's angel child and who didn't like to be shouted at. That little boy said, "Balls your ownself!"

By the loud silence that had come over the room, Bunny realized that he'd gone too far. He looked at his mother, and then at Robert, who avoided meeting his eyes.

His father said sternly, "Go to bed, son. Go right now."

Bunny went over to the sofa, and as he bent down to kiss his mother good-night, his eyes searched her face for the indignation he was sure she felt, and he got a terrible shock: *She was trying to keep from smiling.*

She was not indignant with his father, she was on his father's side.

It was all that he could do to get up the stairs.

II

Bunny woke early to the sound of church bells, though it was Monday morning. Could it be Sunday all over again? Or was there something tremendously the matter?

While he lay in bed, wondering, the sky was split wide open by the whistle from the shoe-factory; by a second whistle from the waterworks. Then the fire alarm began, absorbing whistles and bells into its own dreadful moaning. Until sound became general and the morning throbbed with it.

When Bunny drew his head out from under his pillow Robert was gone, his bed disturbed and empty. One last turn and Bunny got up likewise. Washed himself, dressed, and went downstairs. At the door of the library he waited, uncertain how he might be received. Robert and his mother were eating breakfast

before the fire. His father was sitting in the window
seat, reading the *Chicago Tribune*. His father's coffee
was there neglected on the window sill beside him.
They looked so nice, sitting there. So like themselves.
Was it possible, Bunny considered, that what he remembered about last night had never really happened?

"Good morning, everybody," he said, politely.

All three of them spoke at once:

"The War's over."

"Oh."

In his sleep he dreamed things that were quite
real afterward. Could it have been that? Could he
have dreamed that he talked back to his father and
got sent up to bed? . . . He sat down in his place at
the breakfast table and tied the napkin around his
neck. Last night the music went on for a while without him, and then it stopped abruptly and Robert
came upstairs. That much was true, not something
he dreamed. And through the fringe of his eyelashes
he had watched Robert undressing, taking down the
straps of his wooden leg. Then darkness closed in
around the sides of his bed and he was free to grieve.
If *she* had been the one, he thought—if *she* had been
in trouble, nothing in the world could have kept him
from going to her. She did not really love him . . .
Tears came, hot and effortless. Ran down his cheeks
into the pillow, until he was exhausted and lay quiet,
looking at the wedge of light under the bedroom
door. After a time it grew wider. He heard them
talking downstairs, and then the legs of the card table
creak as they slid into place . . .

PEACE AT LAST

Bunny deciphered the headlines of the morning paper, upside down.

Germany Surrenders
Signs Armistice Terms

"Is that what all the noise is about?"

"Of course. What did you think?" Robert was almost unbearably superior.

"I didn't know. I thought maybe it was a fire."

"A fire! Listen to him. He didn't even know the Armistice is signed!"

Bunny looked to his mother for enlightenment. The word 'Armistice' was new to him, and he felt reasonably certain that Robert didn't know what it meant, any more than he did.

"It means *King's X*," she said.

"It means we beat the Germans," Robert said. He got up from the table and a moment later they heard the front door slam. Robert had gone to join the excitement.

His mother drew him to her. "Haven't you forgotten something?"

Hair? Teeth? Face and hands? He forgot to kiss her . . . In the night someone bent over him where he lay sleeping. Someone put Araminta Culpepper in his arms. She must have . . . Bunny saw that his father was waiting for their attention.

"You might listen to this, son. You might like to remember it when you're grown."

But instead of listening to the military terms of the armistice with Germany, Bunny went and put his head in his mother's lap, for he felt very odd inside of him. He heard her say, "James, this child is burning up with fever!" and he thought dreamily that it must be so. I'm going to be sick, he thought, grateful for the cool hand on his forehead and her nearness. And after that, life was no longer uncertain or incomplete.

Book Two

ROBERT

I

The grass under their feet was trampled and flattened down unevenly. They were hoarse from shouting. They knelt with their hands braced, with their toes balancing. Between their legs they saw the unstable sky

Nine . . .

Sixteen . . .

Thirty-seven . . .

and the roofs of houses.

Offside

Offside
Sixty-four . . .
Offside
Hunderd-and-eighteen-shift
Watch it now
All right
WATCH it
All right
WATCH IT

They ran with knees high and trees spinning. The grey light of evening touched their foreheads, their thin dirt-drawn cheeks, their hands. Crying words, crying names, they fell together—impact of back and shoulder, down, on unknown thighs and the hard ground.

It's your turn to kick off
All right
It's your turn
Three . . .
Seventeen . . .
Thirty-eight . . .
McCarty's offside
Forty-seven . . .
Hang on to it
Hang on to it
Oh . . .
Do you stink, Northway

Into the clear circle of their voices Robert went, limping—McCarty's voice. Northway's voice, taut and protesting. The sky enclosed his shoulders.

Ah

Don't kick it
No
Knock a guy out doing that
What
Fooling like that
Come on
Come on, Morison, pass it
PASS it

Robert was thrown to the ground, alive and breathing.

Touchdown
Listen, after this . . .
Touchdown
It's not, either
For our side
Cryin' out loud
Touchdown
When
Time out I said
When did you
When

Robert picked himself up off the ground and adjusted the knees of his knickerbockers. Not gradually but all at once it was getting dark. He drew his sweater on over his head, weaving argument into it, and denial. They were going home now. Matthews and Scully and Northway and Berryhill (with the ball between his knees) and Engle and McCarty.

So long, McCarty
See you tomorrow
So long

Whose cap is this
So long
Somebody lost his cap
See you tomorrow I said
And don't forget
See you tomorrow

The sky hung down, dark and heavy upon the trees. Robert straddled his bicycle and with Irish between the handlebars left the field, riding now on the sidewalk and now in the street, which was old and full of unexpected hollows. The front wheel of his bicycle turned this way and that, jolting them.

"We should have had that touchdown," Irish said.

"By rights we should have had it, but what can you expect?"

Though it was Robert's bicycle, Matthews or McCarty or Berryhill would have offered to do the pedaling. They took it for granted that Robert wanted them to do the pedaling, on account of his leg. Irish never did. When it was time to go home he came and settled himself between the handle-bars.

After the third long block the car tracks ended and there was level pavement. Street-lights went on at all the intersections. And houses withdrew beyond the rim of the fierce swinging light. Robert, turning, saw the shadow of his head and shoulders lag behind, saw leaves scattering. . . .

After the one-story house of old Miss Talmadge came the Bakers' and the McIntyres' and the Lloyds', then the driveway at the side of Irish's house, and the front walk. Irish got down.

"See you tomorrow."

"Sure, and thank your mother for lunch."

"Sure," Irish said.

There was a light in the kitchen window, but the rest of Irish's house was dark and uninhabitable.

"So long," Robert said.

Irish waited for some leaves to blow past.

"So long."

Through one last street lamp Robert rode alone—the shadow of his wheels elongated, preceding him. Beyond Miss Brew's and the Mitchells' and the Koenigs' (beyond the unseen, undreamed-of darkness) was home: the porch light and the front door, the white pillars along the front of the porch, and Old John waiting in the shadows to greet him.

"How are you, huh? How's the boy?"

Old John wagged in a slow difficult circle, his head and hind quarters and the tip of his tail.

"How's the boy, huh?"

Robert slanted his bicycle against the steps and then, opening the front door, passed into the circumscribed region of the front hall. Irene saw him at once, and started toward him.

"Look out, now." Robert gave her fair warning. "You'll get in trouble!"

If he pretended to go right and went instead to the left, he could always get by his mother. But with Irene it was not so easy.

"Look out, your own self!"

He charged straight at her and was caught, before he could get away. She bent her face down, smothering him.

Standing in the door to the library, his father said, "It is vitally important to keep her out of that boy's room. 'Tie her down,' Dr. Macgregor said, 'if you can't keep her out any other way.' "

Robert found suddenly that he was free.

He pulled off his cap and his outermost sweater. He would go now and stand beside his father, who did not subject him to these humiliating displays of affection. Irene knew he didn't like to be kissed. She only did it for meanness. . . . Robert was confused. The noise of the playing-field was still in his ears, ringing. When he hitched up his knickerbockers, Irene did likewise with her skirt.

"Where's Bunny?" he said, and made a face at her.

"He's sick." It was his father who answered him.

"What's the matter?"

"Spanish influenza," his mother said, coming toward them from the dining-room. Robert turned his eyes away. She was getting big around the waist, on account of the baby coming. He didn't mean to look, but sometimes he did, anyway, and it embarrassed her.

"If I'd only had sense enough," she exclaimed— not to them but to herself, apparently. "If I'd only taken Bunny out of school when the epidemic first started!"

The room seemed very bright to Robert, after being out-of-doors. He could feel the heat from the fireplace through his clothes.

"You can't be taking the boy out of school every time somebody in town gets sick."

"Robert, your hands—" By the way that his mother spoke to him, it was plain that she had not been listening. She roused herself. "You can wash out in the kitchen. Run along now . . . I want to slip upstairs for a minute."

Irene was in the doorway before her.

"I'll go, Bess."

"Thank you just the same, but——"

"I think you'd better let Irene go." His father spoke hurriedly and as if he were not altogether sure that he would be obeyed. Through heat and brightness Robert turned to look at his mother, who would not mind now whether he looked at her or not.

"Why?" she asked.

"Doctor's orders. You're to keep out of Bunny's room."

"But, James, how ridiculous!"

"That's what he said."

While his mother was still hesitating between anger and her original intention, Sophie appeared in the doorway. Sophie had a white apron on. And it seemed to Robert that she and the little brass clock on the mantel struck in unison.

"Dinner," they announced, "is ready."

2

Robert was awakened by a blow at the side of the
house. With sleep still hanging to him, he raised himself tentatively on one elbow. It was daylight, and
Karl's head and shoulders appeared at the window.

"*Wie geht's?*"

Karl had not spoken to any of them in German
since America went into the war, and at first Robert
could not answer him. He knew what the words
meant, but he didn't know where he was until he saw
the sewing-machine and the wire form his mother
used for dressmaking.

"Good, I guess . . . only I don't like sleeping in
this room."

Karl shifted his ladder slightly and peered in
through the screen. It was not safe, they said, for Robert to be in the same room with Bunny. And so they
moved him in here, in the sewing-room, where he had
never slept before. The stairs creaked long after everybody had gone to bed. And the shade snapping kept
him awake.

"I have to, on Bunny's account. He's sick. Did
Sophie tell you?"

Karl nodded, thoughtfully. "That is bad." And
then he smiled—a fine smile that ran off into the grain
of his face.

"Soon I go back!" he said, shifting the ladder.

"Back where?"

"To the old country."

"To Germany? Why are you going to do that?"

Balancing himself, Karl began to take down the screen.

"If you have not seen your father," he said, "if you have not seen your mother, if you have not seen your brothers for seven year . . ."

For Karl to be a German was one thing, it seemed to Robert. That couldn't be helped. But to want to go back there and be with a lot of other Germans was something else again. He yawned.

"How much will you take to close the window?"

With a great display of muscular effort, Karl managed to get the window down half an inch. Then he tucked the screen under his arm and withdrew out of sight. And there was consequently nothing that Robert could do about it, except to kick the covers off and close the window himself. While he dressed, he entertained himself by thinking of the time Aunt Eth came for a visit from Rockford. Irene was there, too. And it was her idea that they put a dress and a hat and a fur neckpiece on the wire dressmaking form and stand it at the head of the stairs to fool his father. Then they waited, snickering, behind the bedroom doors. . . . After the stump sock was on, Robert lifted his artificial leg from the chair, fitted his stump into it, and drew the straps in place over his shoulders. Then, partly standing, partly sitting down, he pulled his knickerbockers on.

Robert's *affliction*, people said, when they thought he wasn't listening.

The breakfast table was set before the fire in the library, as usual. Robert said good-morning to his mother, and to Irene, who was wearing a green silk kimono with yellow flowers on it. They were talking about Bunny.

"Hundred and two," Irene said; "and he complains of pain in his eyes."

Before he had time to unfold his napkin, she turned upon him.

"Stick out your tongue, Robert. I wouldn't be at all surprised— Just as I thought: it's red. It's very red. You must be careful. Just see, Bess——"

But his mother was in no mood for joking. "Here's the cereal," she said, "and sugar and cream. Now shift for yourself."

When Robert was halfway through breakfast there was a blow against the side of the house. He was not startled this time. With his mouth full of toast, he waited until Karl's head and shoulders appeared at the library windows. Then he reflected by turns upon Karl, who was going to Germany; and upon Aunt Eth, who was not like his mother and not like Irene, but in a way rather like both of them. Only she had gray hair, and she was quieter than his mother even, and she taught school in Rockford. When she came to visit, she brought wonderful presents—marbles or a peachy ball-glove for him, and building blocks or a book or paints for Bunny.

Bunny was always either painting or making

something out of blocks. That was all he wanted apparently. He didn't play baseball or marbles or anything that other kids liked to do. At recess time while they were playing games he stood off by himself, waiting for the bell to ring. And if anybody went up to him and started pestering him, instead of hitting back at them, he cried.

Bunny isn't well, his father said. *You have to be careful how you play with him. He isn't as strong as you were when you were his age. . . .* He was careful, all right. But if he took Bunny out to the garage and they had a duel with longswords and daggers, the first crack over the knuckles would send Bunny on his way to the house, bawling. And if they played catch, it was the same thing. (Again the ladder struck, farther on. And Karl's head appeared at the third window. When he was gone Robert reached for the last piece of bacon.) He would have preferred a more satisfactory kind of brother, but since Bunny was the only brother he had, he tried his best to be decent to him. For instance, when Bunny got over the flu he was going to take down his good soldiers from the top of the bookcase and let Bunny look at them.

From this intention he was distracted by his mother, who laid her hand on his sleeve.

"While I think of it, Robert——"

He got up from the table, wiped his mouth with the back of his hand, and on second thought with his napkin. Whenever his mother just remembered something at this time on a Tuesday morning, it was the clean clothes. They came on Saturday, but she never got around to sorting them until it was time to send the soiled ones. If he stopped for Irish and got to school by eight-thirty, as he had promised Scully and Berryhill, he would have to hurry.

The clothes-basket was in the kitchen, on the other side of the stove, where he knew it would be. As he staggered through the library with it, he looked at his mother hopefully. But she was absorbed by what Irene was saying. Robert went on. He made it a practice never to listen to their conversation. It was generally about cooking or clothes, and it made him low in his mind. He set the basket down at the head of the stairs and while he was waiting amused himself by pulling horse-hairs out of the sofa. Irish would be expecting him. They had promised to be at school by eight-thirty, both of them. If he had only known that his mother was going to talk so long. . . . When his patience gave way, he went to the railing and called down.

"Please, will you hurry? I have to go."

His mother called back to him from the library: "All right, Robert. I'm coming." But it was several minutes before she appeared in the downstairs hall. Irene was with her and they were still talking.

"That's the trouble. I never can think of anything for lunch that we haven't already had."

By leaning dangerously far out over the banister, Robert could look down on the tops of their heads. Irene came first. His mother followed, but more slowly.

"Why this unseemly haste?" she asked when she had reached the landing.

"I promised Irish I'd come by for him."

"If that's all it is, then I'm afraid Irish will have to wait."

"Oh, for cryin' out loud!"

"That's enough, Robert."

But it wasn't. It was nowhere near enough, so far as Robert was concerned. "The trouble with you, Mother"—he swallowed hard—"is you don't appreciate what a fine upstanding son you have. I wish you had Harold Engle around the house for about a week. You'd be hop-footing it over to the Engles' so fast, and saying, "We have to have Robert back again, Mrs. Engle. I guess we can't get along without him.""

"I expect I would, Robert."

Mollified, he put the stepladder in place beside the linen-closet.

"Try not to make any more noise than you have to. You'll disturb Bunny."

She bent over the clothes-basket, sorting underwear from pajamas; sorting shirts, napkins, tablecloths, towels. First she handed the sheets up to him, then the pillow-cases. And then she began to sing, under her breath, so that he could scarcely hear what she was singing.

"There's a long long
trail a-
winding
Into the land of

my dreams . . ."
Robert choked on his own haste.
"Where the night-
in-gale is
sing-
ing
And
the
pale——"

The song ended so abruptly that Robert drew his head out from among the sheets and pillowcases to see what was the matter.

"There's a bird in here," Irene exclaimed and went back into the sick-room again, closing the door behind her.

His mother turned to him, her arms filled with winter underwear. "You'll have to do something, Robert."

This was more like it. . . . Robert slid down the stepladder, recklessly, having made up his mind to try the broom first. Then if that didn't work, they'd have to let him use his bee-bee gun.

When he came back upstairs, Irene and his mother were both in Bunny's room—Irene by the dresser and his mother on the edge of Bunny's bed, holding him. With feverish sick eyes, Bunny was watching the sparrow that flew round and round the room in great wide frightened swings. The windows were open as far as they would go.

"It's all on account of Karl taking down the

screens," his mother said. And so far as Robert was concerned, her remark was neither helpful nor necessary. He took hold of the broom.

"You better get out of here, both of you. Because in a minute I'm going to start wielding this!"

Irene retreated at once, laughing and covering her hair with her hands as the bird brushed by her. His mother was not so easily hurried. "Lie still, lover," she said, with the bird flying from one side of the room to the other, swooping, turning, diving intently past her face. The door closed and right away Bunny was sitting up again, his eyes glittering with fever.

"Please don't hurt it, Robert!"

"Why not?"

Robert swung vigorously.

"Because I don't want you to."

"One sparrow more or less—"

"I don't care, I don't want you to hurt it!"

Robert swung and missed again. Nevertheless, the bird dropped and lay like a stone on the counterpane of Bunny's bed. As Robert's hand closed over it, he remembered: *It is vitally important to keep her out of that boy's room. . . .*

"I'll tell Mother on you!"

Tears ran down Bunny's cheeks.

Tie her down, the doctor said. . . . The sparrow escaped from Robert's fingers and with a sudden twist shot through the open window.

Tie her down . . .

And already she had managed to get in when they were all excited. Already she had been sitting on the edge of Bunny's bed.

"Oh, shut up!" Robert said, and swung his broom upon the empty air.

3

All Thursday morning Robert raked leaves—raked them toward him until there was a crisp pile at his feet, and then another and another. With no more leaves to fall, the trees stood out in bare essential form, forgotten during the summer and now remembered. By noon the yard was swept clean on both sides of the house, and he had carried the trash up from the basement. There was nothing left but to burn the dead leaves and trash together, in the alley. And he could do that whenever he liked.

As soon as lunch was over, Robert went upstairs to get his football helmet and jersey. He was almost at the front door when his mother saw him.

"Where are you going?"

"To play football." He had done all that his father told him to do. The afternoon belonged to him. It was as good as in his pocket. "The whole gang——"

"I want to talk to you a minute."

His mother went on into the living-room and adjusted one of the shades which was not on a line with the others.

"Come here," she said.

"What's the matter?" he demanded suspiciously.

"I want to see what makes you bulge so."

"That's handkerchieves."

"One, two, three, four . . . So I begin to perceive. Your back pocket must be a place where they meet and congregate. Suppose you take them up to the hamper in the back hall, where they belong."

"Do I have to do it now? Can't I do it later?"

"If you like. But I'm afraid you can't play football this afternoon."

"Why not?"

"Various reasons. I want you to stay in your own yard, do you hear? Because if you run all over town, you'll be playing with all kinds of boys who probably haven't a thing the matter with them."

Robert looked at his mother unguardedly. She was smiling, but what she said wasn't funny and in fact didn't make a bit of sense. They had been up with Bunny for two nights—first Irene and then his father. And today was the third day, so that his fever would break, Dr. Macgregor said, or else it would go higher.

"I'm not going all over town. I'm only going to the vacant lot across from Dowlings' to play football."

"Please don't argue with me, Robert."

Don't argue with her! And already they were choosing up sides. As plainly as if he were there, Robert could hear them: Scully and Matthews and Northway and Berryhill.

"Crimenently——"

"There's no point in discussing it any further, Robert. Just do as I say."

His mother was tired. That was the whole trouble. She was tired and she didn't realize. . . . Robert went into the library and sat down. His father was there with stacks of papers around him—work that he had brought home from the office. He was vaguely aware of Robert's presence but no more, and for that Robert was grateful, because there was a lump in his throat that he couldn't seem to dispose of. He twirled his football helmet this way and that on the end of his finger, and tried not to think about things.

Partly it was all his own fault, because he let his mother into the room where Bunny was, so maybe it was right for him to be punished. Two days had passed and she didn't look any different, but maybe it was right anyway. Only what good, he asked himself as he got up and went over to the rocking-chair—what good was it having school closed? What good was all the time in the world? So long as he had to stay in his own yard, what good was anything?

No answer occurred to him, and therefore he rocked—gently at first, then with conviction.

> *"She was goin' downgrade*
> *Makin' ninety miles an hour*
> *When the whis-sul broke out*
> *In a scream (Beep-Beep!).*
> *He was found in the wreck*
> *With his hand on the throttle*

All scalded to death
With steam . . ."

Rocking and singing cheerfully, Robert was
well into the second verse when his father took a
pencil from behind his ear and said, "If you're going
to stay in the house, you'll have to be quiet, son. I can't
concentrate."

Robert jammed the football helmet on his head
and went to the kitchen, where Sophie was washing
the sheets for Bunny's bed. Sophie was always disagreeable lately. She flew around with her nose in the
air, bossing everybody. And if he so much as asked for
a piece of bread and butter, she would threaten to tell
his mother on him.

"Now what do you want?"

"Last night's paper."

"Right there under the table. And don't get the
rest of them in a mess, do you hear?"

People were always saying, *Do you hear, Robert? Do you hear me?* As if there was something
wrong with his ears. But there wasn't. He heard everything that he wanted to hear and a lot more besides.
The newspaper was on top. He folded it carefully and
tucked it under his belt.

"What do you want last night's paper for?"

"None of your beeswax," he said, and slammed
the door on his way out.

Old John followed him around to the back of the
house, where the roof sloped down over the cellar
stairs. There, by bracing his arms against two box el-

ders which grew side by side, Robert could get up on
the roof. As soon as he put his knee up, Old John
whined.

"You better go somewhere else and play," Robert said, bitterly, and drew his other leg up after him.

Once he got as far as the kitchen roof, the rest
was easy. Up there he was no longer at the mercy
of anybody who chose to take a pencil from behind
his ear, or raise or lower a window shade. He could
look down on everything—on the back yard and the
garage and the fence and the alley behind the fence,
on Burnhams' trash pile and the row of young maples
along the other side of the alley. To the right he could
see the garden, the grape arbor, and the yard. To the
left was the drive, and Bunny's sandpile under a big
tree. Robert surveyed the whole scene carefully, before he sat down with his back against the chimney
and opened the *Courier*. Page two. . . . There it was:
"*SCHOOLS . . . The school board and the health
officer have posted notices on the school houses and at
places about town to the effect that the schools will be
closed until further notice . . .*" Robert felt very
small prickles in the region of his spine. He read the
first sentence twice, to make sure that there had not
been a mistake. . . . His mother couldn't keep him at
home indefinitely. Things as awful as that didn't happen. She was just tired and cross this afternoon. And
so there would be time for playing football and marbles, for making shinny sticks, for taking muskrat
traps down from the top of the garage and cleaning
them, for hunting rabbits and squirrels. . . . But

there was more in the notice than that. It meant that
something was happening in town, all around him.
Not an open excitement like the day the Armistice
was signed, with fire engines and whistles and noise
and people riding around in the hearse. But a quiet
thing that he couldn't see or hear; that was in Bunny's
room, and on Tenth Street where Arthur Cook lived,
and more places than that. Far down inside him, and
for no reason that he could understand, Robert was
pleased. . . . *The notice reads as follows: To the Par-
ents . . . While the epidemic has not reached Logan
to any extent, and while it may seem unnecessary to
many, yet after consulting with the health officer and
the medical authorities your school board decided to
close the schools for this week at least, in the hope
that no new cases will develop and that this community will be spared any serious epidemic. The Illinois
committee on public safety strongly advises this course
and cautions people against gathering in large num-
bers for any purpose, also traveling on railroad trains
except when absolutely necessary. . . .* Robert closed
his eyes. It seemed once more as if he could hear
shouting. *First down and . . . four . . . to go . . .*
Matthews and Berryhill shouting. And for that reason
he wished (just for this afternoon) that Bunny, who
was sick, anyway, had been the one to get run over
and have his leg cut off above the knee.

But it was Crazy Jake that Robert heard, coming down the alley with his wagon and his old white
horse. A long time ago, before Robert was born,
Crazy Jake was held up by robbers who took his

money from him and his watch, and hit him over the head. And because he was never able to think very well after that, he drove through alleys collecting tin cans for people. And he came at all hours. Robert had heard his mother say that lying awake sometimes in the middle of the night, she heard him.

"Hi, Jake!"

That was the thing about being on the roof. Robert could see Crazy Jake, who couldn't see him. It was like being invisible. Searching steadily, Crazy Jake emptied the Morisons' ashcan into his wagon. Then with his lips blowing, with his vacant face pressed to the sky, he drove on.

There was still part of the roof for Robert to climb—the upper level which extended out in the shape of a ledge. To reach it he made use of the rainspout, the window frame, and the iron hook where the screen had been fastened. When he reached the top he was out of breath and a little dizzy with his accomplishment. The distance to the ground was considerable; enough to affect the pit of his stomach. He could reach out if he wanted to. He could almost touch the branches of the box elder. But also he might fall headlong and break every bone in his body. And they would all come running out of the house. His mother . . . she would cry and take on about *him*, for a change. But she couldn't do anything. It would be too late. . . . Sometimes Robert fell from the roof of the garage, sometimes from the top of the flag-pole at the Chautauqua grounds. But in any case, people came running and took on over him.

At two o'clock Dr. Macgregor's car drove up before the Morisons' house. Until he could slip out of the grooves of his day-dream, Robert thought that Dr. Macgregor must be coming up the walk to see him. Then he remembered. It was Bunny who was sick, and this was the second time that Dr. Macgregor had come since morning.

Robert would have called out to him if he had dared. But he was not supposed to climb on this part of the roof, and they might hear him, inside. That was the trouble, he said to himself. Whenever they got into a state, it was always on Bunny's account. They never had doctors for him. Not since he was run over.

It would be nice if his father read in the paper about a specialist who had discovered a way to make bones grow. Not really, of course. Because there wasn't any way to make bones grow, after they were once cut off. But just supposing. . . . They would take him to Chicago to see the specialist. And after looking him over pretty carefully the specialist would tell his father and mother to take him home again and put him to bed in a dark room with the shades pulled down. Only, before they did that they'd better go out to Lincoln Park and see the animals.

After he had been home a week his leg would be put in a special cast, made of elastic plaster. They would have a nurse for him, of course. And nobody else could come into the room unless he asked for them. And maybe for days and days he wouldn't ask for them. Just lie there and take dark green—no, dark *purplish* medicine through a glass tube, every hour and a half.

And the nurse's name would be Miss Walker.

At the end of a week the specialist would come and measure the outside of the cast, which would have expanded maybe the fraction of an inch. His mother would cry, and they'd have to take her out of the room. Or maybe it had better be Irene. Because his mother wasn't very easily upset. And the specialist would tell them he had to lie flat, that was the main thing. Lie flat on his back and not talk to anybody but Miss Walker (who was starched but not skinny, like the nurse that looked after him when he had his accident). Miss Walker was interested in football, so they talked about that, mostly. . . . Absorbed in these imaginary matters, Robert sat so still that the sparrows returned to fight with one another above the kitchen chimney. . . . When his stump began to hurt, they called the specialist by long-distance. He came and measured the cast and said it was all right: the stump was supposed to hurt. It was supposed to hurt now because the knee was forming. Within a month's time, he said, Robert would have a new knee.

The new medicine was red and thick like cod-liver oil, and the first spoonful made Robert sick. For a while they had to give it to him with orange juice. But then he learned to hold his nose and swallow it right down while Miss Walker said *That's the stuff*.

The cast began to get wider as flesh formed about the new bone. And the bone was growing, though it took time. He had to be patient and not think about it, because after a while the stump would begin to hurt again. And when it got to the foot, the specialist said it would hurt most of all.

Everything worked out just that way.

When it came time for them to remove the cast, they took him to the hospital. Dr. Macgregor was there—no, that was not right. There would be several doctors with masks on. Dr. Macgregor would give the anesthetic and the last thing he would remember would be Dr. Macgregor telling him to take deep breaths so they could hurry up and get it over with. . . . Sections here and there needed polishing, Robert decided. The end, especially, where he woke up and felt with his hand, through the covers. But on the whole it would do. At least until there was time to go over it.

For it was late in the afternoon. The sky all around him had lost its brightness and some of its color. And the heat had gone out of the tin roof, when he put his hands against it. Like an explorer long out of touch with the world, he advanced to the edge and looked down. Irene was there in the garden, alone.

There were signs, he told himself. If Irene had come outside now, it must mean something. Bunny's fever had broken. Or perhaps, as Dr. Macgregor said, it had gone higher. Slipping and sliding much of the way, Robert went down to find out. When he reached the box elders, Irene turned and started toward the kitchen door. She did not see him, apparently. She was going inside. He opened his mouth to call to her, but some one else did. Some one called her by her name, in a voice that Robert had not heard for years.

"Irene . . ."

The gate swung open, at the back of the garden, and Boyd Hiller came inside. He passed so close by the box elders that Robert saw grey hair at his temples, and his grey unhappy eyes.

"Irene, I've been waiting out there for hours. I couldn't go away—not without seeing you!"

Robert saw and understood everything, even the queer tightness in his side, which was jealousy. And the tears that sprang into his eyes. Irene had come out into the garden to meet Boyd Hiller, and Boyd Hiller would ask her to go back to him. And if she did that, Robert wouldn't want to see her again. Not ever, he said to himself as he escaped between the trees and around the corner of the house. Not as long as he lived.

4

After dinner Robert had the library all to himself. His father and mother went upstairs immediately, but he did not join them, for fear of meeting Irene. With no homework to do, he ran his fingers along the top shelf of the bookcase and drew out *The Scottish Chiefs*. It was an old edition that had belonged to his Grandfather Blaney. The paper had turned yellow around the edges, and the print was small. But it began the way Robert liked books to begin, and by the second page he was submerged. The lamp cord was his only means of contact with the upper air. He clung to that, and shaped the words in silence as he read.

At eight o'clock his mother came downstairs and stood in the doorway a moment, looking at him. He did not know that she was there. Nor did he know when Dr. Macgregor came for the third time since morning. Robert was crossing the bridge at Lanark and saw the rising moon. Committed to him, as the worthiest of Scots, was the iron box which the false Baliol had given to Lord Douglas, and Douglas to Monteith. And he had five long miles to go before he could reach the glen of Ellerslie.

At ten o'clock Irene came and took the book away from him. He was too dazed; he had been too long in another world to remember that he had been avoiding her.

"It's time for you to go to bed."

"Who said so?"

"Your ancient and honorable father."

Robert pulled himself up out of the chair. If it had been his mother, he could have finished the part he was reading and maybe gone on into the next chapter to see what was happening there. But his father was different.

With men and horses moving beside him, Robert made his way up the stairs to the sewing-room, undressed, and got into bed. For the first time he perceived how still the house was, how full of waiting. When he was little, he used to be afraid of the dark. He used to think that unnamable things were about to spring out at him from behind doors. Sometimes it was merely the house itself, tense and expectant, that frightened him. He was not afraid any longer.

He could hear voices—Irene and Dr. Macgregor and the sound of Irene's heels striking the stair. While he was waiting for her to come up again, he fell asleep.

It was still dark outside when he awoke. And no way that he could tell how late it was, or how early. Poised between sleep and waking, he got up to go to the bathroom. What he saw then when he hopped out into the hall was like a picture, and remained that way in his mind long afterward. There were lights burning everywhere, in all the rooms. At the head of the stairs Irene and his mother were standing with their backs to him. Because neither of them moved, Robert could not move; until Bunny raised up in bed quite calmly and said, "What time is it?"

Dr. Macgregor appeared from the bedroom across the hall and went into Bunny's room at once. When he came out again, his face was relaxed and smiling.

"Elizabeth," he said, "your angel child is going to get well."

5

The next few days were like a party, it seemed to Robert. There were cut flowers from the greenhouse and callers every afternoon. And Sophie had to spend most of her time running back and forth with the teapot.

All his mother's friends came to see her—"Aunt" Amelia, "Aunt" Maud, "Aunt" Belle—and stayed often until the stroke of six. Robert could not remember when the library had been so full of women drinking tea and talking about necklines. Or when his mother had been more happy, more like herself.

"Having a baby," she said to him privately, "is no worse than spring house-cleaning. It isn't even as bad. You don't have to take the curtains down."

He was not allowed to go out of the yard, and Irish couldn't come there and play. But one way and another (letting him stay up later, having his favorite desserts, listening to what he had to say about the high school football team) his mother made it up to him, so that after a while he didn't really mind.

What she wanted, apparently, was to make things up to everybody. She paid the paper boy six weeks in advance. And nothing would do but that old Miss Atkins, who came every Saturday with Boston brown bread and potholders (there were stacks of them in the linen closet), must stay to lunch. And the best blue china must be brought out for her.

Sophie alone was red-eyed and disagreeable. Robert and his mother agreed that it was on account of Karl. It was because Karl was going back to Germany.

"What I don't see," Robert explained, "is why she doesn't go to Germany with him."

"Perhaps she would," his mother said, "if Karl asked her to."

"Why does he have to *ask* her to?"

"For the looks of things."

"Couldn't she ask *him?*"

"She could but she won't."

"Then why doesn't she just go by herself?"

"That's what I'm afraid of. Whatever you do, don't put that idea in her head. It might be years before I could get some one to make as decent pie-crust as Sophie does."

"No," Robert said, gloomily, "I won't."

"As for *our* going away, that's arranged now— everything but the railroad tickets. And I do believe that with the least encouragement your father would go right down and get them. You know how he likes to have everything ready beforehand. . . . The only thing I have to do is to make sure that the baby is a girl. I don't care, particularly. I *like* scissors and snails and puppy-dogs' tails. But your father has his heart set on a girl. And if it turns out to be another boy, we may have to send it back. There's no telling. . . . Irene is going to stay with you and Bunny at night, so that you won't be alone. . . . If anything comes up, you're to call Dr. Macgregor. Only you're not to bother him unless it's something important—unless, for example, the house is on fire, or you catch Sophie upstairs trying on my hats. Do you understand? . . . You're old enough, Robert, to take on responsibility, the way your father is always saying. And by that I mean it would be a good thing if you'd change your underwear from time to time, and not leave the light burning in the basement. . . . Also I want you to

look after Bunny while we're gone. See that he goes
to bed early even if you have to go when he does. He's
been through such a siege, you know. . . . And that
he eats the things he's supposed to eat, not just meat
and potatoes. . . . And you're to write once a
week, and brush your teeth night and morning, and
not make any more trouble for Irene than you have
to. . . . And while I think of it, how do you like the
name *Jeanette—Jeanette Morison*—for a little girl?"

With his mother Robert was almost never con-
strained or ill at ease. It seemed easy and natural for
her to be talking about whatever it was that was on
her mind. She didn't stop what she was doing. Hardly
ever. And that way he felt free to tell her all sorts of
things. Because he always knew that she would go
right on sorting the sheets and pillowcases.

But with his father it was different. He liked his
father and he liked pretty much the same things his
father liked. Old clothes, baseball talk, fishing, guns,
automobiles, tinkering. When they were out in the
country, his father and he turned to look at the same
things. His mother liked trees and sunsets, but *they*
liked horses plowing, orchards, and fine barns. They
even liked the same kind of food, and put salt on
everything, regardless. But if he came up behind his
father and started to tell him something, he was always
sorry afterward. It was never the way he had hoped it
would be.

His father's comments embarrassed him. *I'm glad
you told me, son. But now the best thing is to forget
that as quick as you can. If you want to grow up to*

*be decent and self-respecting, you haven't time for
any foul-minded talk like that.* . . . Or, out of a clear
sky his father would say *Remember now, it doesn't
make any difference what kind of trouble you run
into; your father will always be right here.* . . .
Something that Robert knew perfectly well. And that
somehow there was no need for saying.

Or else it was something that he didn't want to
know. Like the time they were alone in the living-
room and his father said, "I expect you've been wondering, Robert, why your mother has to go all the
way to Decatur to have the baby—why she can't have
it here at home. There's a reason, of course. A very
good one."

Robert had taken it for granted that his father
would not talk about *that*. . . . And he had not been
wondering why they were going to Decatur, because
mostly his father and mother didn't tell him why they
did things and so he had long ago stopped wondering.

"When you were born, your mother had a pretty
difficult time of it. There were several days when it
didn't look as though she would pull through. And
then Bunny came along, and it was the same thing.
But there's a doctor in Decatur, a very fine specialist,
who's developed a new treatment in dealing with
childbirth. I could explain it to you, but the upshot is
that Dr. Macgregor thinks we ought to take her over
there, even at considerable expense."

"I see."

When Robert stood up to go his father laid the
evening paper aside and stood up also.

"Because it's a pretty serious thing," his father said, and put his arm rather awkwardly around Robert's shoulder.

Together they paced, slowly, and without reason, from one end of the living-room to the other. After a time Robert began to feel the weight of his leg. He had only to say something about it and his father would stop, of course. But that would have meant giving in—admitting that there was something the matter with him.

So far as his mother was concerned, there wasn't anything the matter with him. If they were out fishing and had to crawl through a barbed-wire fence, his father looked back sometimes. Or called over his shoulder, *Can you make it, sport?* . . . But his mother went right on. She was like Irish in that respect.

And the same way with games. His mother took it for granted that he would learn to swim and dive, so he did. And everything that other boys did. And the only time she praised him was when he won the tennis singles at the Scout camp. The Scoutmaster was surprised and said how fine it was—meaning that Robert was handicapped with only one leg. And the news got into the paper, eventually, and his mother wrote: *Very nice. Mailed your clean underwear this a.m. Are you getting enough to eat?*

Robert had the post card still. He kept it in a box, with his second-class Scout badge and his arrowheads.

"Things are going to be different now," his father was saying. "You'll have to do more for yourself. With a baby in the house you can't expect people to be picking up your things after you and keeping your clothes in order."

Once they went out into the hall solemnly. And once into the library. And so long as neither of them spoke, Robert could imagine that he knew what was going on in his father's mind; that they understood each other. But to have his father turn on him and say, "These things happen to everybody, sooner or later. We have to expect them," was altogether shocking. Robert looked around wildly as they bore down on the walnut sofa. They turned aside, of course, at the very last minute, but it was a narrow escape.

"Your mother is a fine woman," his father said.

6

Bunny was very pale after his illness, and he tired easily. The first time that he was allowed to come downstairs was an event. Robert got out his soldiers and laid the box on Bunny's knees.

The box was so large that it was all Bunny could do to hold it. And Robert stood by, in case Bunny should want to take the soldiers out of their places. When Bunny had looked at them a short while (at the lancers with silver breastplates and silver plumes, the cowboys, the Cossacks on white horses with bear-skin caps and rifles slung across their backs) he indicated that Robert could put the lid on. His hands shook slightly, and there was satisfaction in his tired eyes.

"They're nice," he said. "Thank you, Robert. Thank you a lot." And then "Maybe sometime we could play with them together?"

Robert didn't answer.

"You take half and I take half, and then we could have a battle—how would that be?"

Robert returned the soldiers to the top of the bookcase where they belonged. He wanted to be nice to Bunny because Bunny had been sick. But on the other hand, it wouldn't do to commit himself.

He said, "Maybe we could sometime," and went on to the living-room to practice his music lesson. Because there was an epidemic, his mother said, was no reason why he should get off practicing.

For a while—for fifteen minutes, perhaps—he practiced conscientiously. Then he made a series of trips out to the front hall to look at the clock. Each time that he came back he devoted considerable attention to the piano stool, which was either too high to suit him; or else too low. With half an hour still before him, he switched from *The Shepherd Boy's Prayer* to

Go tell
That was wrong——
Go tell
Aunt Rho
die her——

"Flat, Robert . . . B Flat!" his mother called from somewhere, from the butler's pantry. She was eating again. . . . That was the trouble. If they'd just leave him alone, he'd get along fine and maybe learn to play the piano so well that he could give recitals and people would have to pay money to come and hear him. Instead of that, they jumped on him— his mother jumped on him every time he struck a wrong note, so that he was always having to go back to the beginning, hour after hour, week after week, year in (he said to himself) and year out.

When he went again to see what time it was, Irene was standing in front of the pier-glass. She was poking long hatpins into her hat, and he tried to slip away while her back was turned. Nevertheless, she saw him in the mirror and stopped him. And this time it was not a matter of being kissed.

"What," she said, "did you think of my caller?"

Robert could think of nothing in reply, so he sat down on the bottom step of the stairs. When Irene was convinced that her hat was straight, she came and sat down beside him.

"I guess I didn't think anything," he said.

"That's a likely story."

Irene took his hand and covered the skinned knuckles with her own. Robert considered a place in his trousers knee—a place which was about worn through. The trouble was that he couldn't tell Irene what he thought about her caller—not really. Besides, it wouldn't make any difference. If she was going to live with Boyd Hiller again, she'd do it regardless of anything he said.

Long ago, before he was hurt and almost before

he could remember, there was a wedding in the Episcopal church, with lots of people. It was after dark and they went there in a taxicab—Irene and Grandfather Blaney. And Irene was afraid that he'd drop the ring if he carried it on a pillow, so she put it in his hand and closed his fingers over it. That much he remembered. And going down the aisle past all the people.

But there was more afterward. It was one of the family stories that he had heard over and over, until it seemed to him that he could almost remember it. When the time came for the ring, he wouldn't give it up. Boyd tried to take it from him and he said *No, it's Eenie's ring!* So loud that people heard him all over the church.

"The honest truth, Robert . . ."

Irene had to turn, they said, and take the ring away from him. But that part he didn't remember.

". . . the honest truth is that I didn't know Boyd was coming. I knew he was in town, of course. And when I took little Agnes to her Grandmother Hiller's, I saw him and talked to him for a few minutes. That was all."

Robert was not used to having grown-up people confide in him. First his father, and now Irene. . . . His mouth stiffened with embarrassment.

"I had been in the house all afternoon, you know, with Bunny. And your father came up to relieve me, so I threw a shawl around my shoulders and went outside to get a breath of air. . . . When I discovered who it was, Robert, I did the same thing you did—I ran away."

A week's suspense, a week of secret misery escaped in one breath, so that Robert felt very light and unstable. It wasn't that Boyd Hiller was to blame for his accident—because he wasn't, really. He didn't know that Robert was climbing on the back end of his carriage. He didn't even know that Robert was there until Robert got his foot in the wheel. And then it was too late. . . . He thought of that every time that he saw Boyd. He couldn't help thinking of that. But what troubled him now was something else. It was about Irene.

"The older you get, Robert, the less courage you have."

Robert stood up and put his hands in his pockets. He was glad of one thing, anyway. He would not have to avoid Irene any longer.

"You wouldn't like to see some muskrat traps, would you?"

"Not now. The taxi will be here any minute."

Robert glanced at the clock. They had already talked away six whole minutes of practicing.

"Next time, then?"

Irene buttoned her right glove and drew the left one on—all but the thumb. "Next time," she said, and kissed him soundly on the mouth.

7

Robert awoke into a bright cold room. There was snow on the window sill, and on the floor beneath. He looked out and saw that the walks were gone, the roofs buried under an inch of snow. And in the level morning light, which came neither from the sky nor the white earth but from somewhere between sky and earth, the maples stood out with stereoscopic clarity.

While Robert was trying to accustom himself to the change, his mother came in.

"I never knew it to fail," she announced as she closed the window.

"Never knew what to fail?"

"Sophie——"

Although it was a thing he had seen happen a thousand times, Robert sat up in bed and watched his mother turn on the radiator.

"She's gone and had all her teeth out. Every tooth in her head. Wouldn't you know! She came to work this morning feeling so miserable and she was such a sight, that I told her to go home. . . ."

The radiator began to kick and stomp, and only occasionally could Robert make out a word or two of what his mother was saying. When she left, he washed and dressed slowly. For long periods at a time his mind remained stationary and entranced, while he played with the buttons on his shirt. But there were moments in between, when he thought about teeth, and how he swallowed one at the age of seven; and about his Grandmother Morison, who had false teeth and kept them in a glass of water at night; and about Sophie, and what she would look like without any.

Eventually the smell of bacon frying aroused him. He went downstairs by the back way, and found his mother in the kitchen.

"Was it that," he said, "that was making Sophie so disagreeable?"

"I don't know."

His mother turned the gas down under the coffee-pot.

"I didn't ask her. She was in no fit condition. If she had been, I'd have found out where she keeps the grapefruit knife. Because I've looked high and low. . . ."

After breakfast Robert wandered upstairs and stood looking at the back room that was some day to be his.

No change had been made since the day he came here with his mother and they planned together what they were going to do to fix it up. His mother suggested matting for the floors, in place of rugs. And pictures of birds. Also if they could pick up an old sea-chest somewhere—a chest that opened from the top. He thought it would be a good idea if the bed were built against the wall like a seaman's bunk, high and narrow, with long drawers under it where he could keep his things. There was to be a bulletin board where he could tack up notices and post-cards that he wanted to look at. And they both agreed that the door was to have a padlock on it.

Now that everything was so upset, with the baby coming and all, he couldn't expect them to do much about his room. Not for a while, anyway. Turning to go, he noticed the arrangement of rectangular walls and buildings: the ruler, the block of stone, brown paper, pencils, wooden spools. Bunny must have built it—whatever it was. He was the only one who ever came here. But Robert saw that with that piece of cardboard braced against the sides of the two largest buildings and curving upward he could construct a first-rate airplane hangar.

He carried out his idea immediately, and in a way that satisfied him beyond words. But he could not resist making one or two more serious changes, and he became so intent on what he was doing that he was startled when he heard Bunny's voice, close behind him: "What's that?"

"A flying field."

Bunny regarded him with suspicion.

"What did you think it was?"

Robert leaned back proudly, so that Bunny could see his handiwork. It was all neatly arranged—the hangar and three sheds, the road leading up to it, the corners of the field. He saw that Bunny, too, was pleased, or at least hovering on the edge of pleasure.

"Those are searchlights," he said, fearing that Bunny would miss them.

Bunny was looking at something else—at a cylindrical box which had once contained a typewriter ribbon.

"My village . . . you've torn up my Belgian village!"

Robert sighed. All he ever wanted to do was to play with Bunny. And whatever he did, the result was always the same.

"It can be fixed, Bunny. All you have to do is build it over again."

"It can't, either. And I wasn't through with it. I was going to play with it a lot more and now you've spoiled it!" Bunny looked so queer when he lost his temper: white as a sheet and like a little old man. "You've spoiled the whole thing."

"I know, Bunny, but I didn't mean to. . . . And I built you a new flying-field, didn't I? That's a lot better than any old Belgian village."

"If you'd only play with your own things," Bunny shouted, "and keep out of here where you don't belong . . ." Blocks, kindling-wood, pencils, wooden spools scattered noisily across the floor and out into the hall where his father stood, looking at them.

"What's all this?"

"My village. Robert went and——"

"I didn't, either. I didn't spoil anything. I was just——"

"Be quiet, both of you. And listen to what I have

to say. Irene *was* going to stay with you but she's out of town."

"Where did she go?"

"Chicago."

"What for?"

"I don't know. You'll have to ask her. Sophie is in no fit shape to come to work, and so I've been talking to your Aunt Clara. You and Bunny are to go there and stay while we're gone."

As suddenly as that, everything was changed. Everything was different.

Robert was too uneasy to remain upstairs even while his clothes were being packed, and so he wandered disconsolately from room to room, with Bunny at his heels. Bunny was looking for his yellow agate which had got lost somehow, or mislaid. And he seemed to be more perturbed about that than he was over the change of plans.

For some time Robert stood before the bookcase in the library, uncertain whether or not to take his soldiers. He didn't want to go and stay at Aunt Clara's. He didn't like it there. But on the other hand, what if the house should burn down while they were gone. . . . At the last minute he decided to take both his soldiers and *The Scottish Chiefs*, which he had finished once, and read partly a second time.

"Hurry up, son," his father said from the doorway. "Dr. Macgregor is outside with his car, waiting. Say good-by to your mother and then we'll. . . ."

When Robert came into the hall his mother was standing before the pier-glass with her hat and coat on.

He started toward her, but Bunny was there first, tugging at her and sobbing wildly into her neck.

"Why," she exclaimed through her veil. "Crying . . . at your age. What a thing to have happen!" And when Bunny cried the harder, "There, there, angel, don't take on so!"

Robert hesitated. He saw his father pull out his watch.

"Well, good-by," he said, though she probably didn't hear him. "Good-by, Mother. Take care of yourself." And went on out to the car.

8

Aunt Clara was waiting for them behind the storm door.

"Well, how are my boys? And how are you, Doctor?"

Robert held his breath while she embraced him. Aunt Clara was a large woman—almost as tall as his father. And on weekdays she didn't wear any corset.

"Won't you take your coat off, Doctor? I say won't you take your coat off?"

Dr. Macgregor set their suitcases down in the front hall.

"Not today, thank you."

"When James called, I told him to bring the children right over. Mr. Paisley and I were going to Vandalia for Thanksgiving, but with the epidemic and so many people sick and all, we decided to stay home."

Blindfolded and set down like the suitcases in Aunt Clara's front hall, Robert would have known where he was. He would have known mostly by the smell, which was not like the smell of any house that he had ever been in, and not easy to describe, except that it was something like the smell of clothes shut up in boxes for too long a time.

The walls and the woodwork were dark, and the shades always at half-mast, except in the parlor, where they were all the way down, to keep the rug from fading.

While Robert stood with his cap and his overcoat still on, it occurred to him that he might slip out the back door and around the house to the car again, before anybody noticed what he was doing. He could stay with Dr. Macgregor until his father and mother came home, and then everything would be all right. He moved toward the dining-room, but just then Dr. Macgregor put his hand out to say good-by.

"If there is anything you want," Dr. Macgregor said; "if anything comes up, Robert—"

Aunt Clara answered for him: "If there's any occasion to, Doctor, we'll call you. I say we'll call you."

It was clear from the tone of her voice that there would be no occasion. In the doorway, with cold air rushing in between his legs, Dr. Macgregor turned and smiled at Robert approvingly. "Be good boys," he said, and closed the door behind him.

"Well," Aunt Clara said, "I wasn't looking for

you quite so soon. Half after nine, your father said. Go stand your overshoes on the register, Robert. There's snow on them and it'll stain the carpet."

Robert had intended to watch until Dr. Macgregor drove away, but he did not dare go to the window when Aunt Clara had told him to do something else. He stood bravely still, however. For they were rubbers, not overshoes. And in the second place, Aunt Clara was not his mother. He didn't have to mind her. Unless he wanted to, he didn't have to do anything she said.

"Come upstairs with me, Bunny. I'll take the spread off, and the bolster, in Grandma's room. And then you can have some place to lie down. You must be careful for a while. You've been a sick boy."

Although his face was streaked with tears, Bunny was pleased with himself. Robert recognized the symptoms. And he saw that Bunny was making up to Aunt Clara—starting up the stairs in front of her as if she were the one person that he liked and depended on. Just as he did to Irene, or to Sophie, or to anybody who happened to be around and could get him what he wanted. When Bunny and Aunt Clara reached the landing, Robert went over to the register and stood on it, rubbers and all, preserving his independence by a kind of technicality while the hot air came up in waves, around his legs.

As soon as the rubbers were dry he took them off and his overcoat and cap, and went into the darkened parlor. He was looking for a place to put his soldiers. Though it was safe, or fairly so, the parlor would not do because it was never used except for company. Then Aunt Clara raised the shades halfway and people sat about in the big mahogany rocking-chairs, making conversation. On the piano there was a seashell that roared and a big starfish that came apart, once, in Robert's hands. He could still remember how he felt, holding it and trying to make the broken point stay on. Eventually, in fright, he put the starfish back the way it was, on top of the piano, and hoped that no one would notice. Aunt Clara discovered it the very next day, when she came to dust, and said would he please not touch things without asking.

All Robert wanted was to see what it looked like underneath. But if he had known what was going to happen, he would have let the starfish be.

In the sitting-room over the two doorways were plaster heads—a Negress in a red turban, and another (darker, and larger by several sizes) in a blue. Robert could never make up his mind whether he liked them or whether he didn't. And so he sat experimentally in various parts of the room, on the leather couch, in the big chair, holding his box of soldiers. Wherever he went, the Negresses followed him with their white eyes. He asked his mother once where Aunt Clara got them, and she said in darkest Africa. But that was only his mother's way of saying things. Aunt Clara had been to New York with Uncle Wilfred, and come home by way of Niagara Falls. And she had been to Omaha, to a funeral. But she had never crossed the ocean. Robert was quite sure of that. Just as he was sure that the heads were not real heads but plaster, and the fireplace not a real fireplace, though it had a fancy metal screen that looked as if it were screwed on over a grate.

One time when Aunt Clara was away at a meeting of the Ladies Aid, he took the screws out and discovered that there was nothing behind it but the wall. Only the metal screen wouldn't go back on again. He tried all afternoon until his mother came to get him, and still he couldn't make the screws stay in. But it was all right, because his mother told Aunt Clara to have a man come out and fix it, and she'd pay for it. And on the way home she wasn't even angry with him. For years, she said, she'd been wanting to do the very same thing.

For his part, Robert liked things to be whatever they were. And he liked them to work. Having reached that conclusion, he went and stood before the bookcase, helplessly interested by all the curious objects that he saw there, and that he was never allowed to touch—the coral, the starfish, the shells, the peacock feather, the parrot eggs, the ocarina, the colored stones. When he could not bear to look at them any longer, he turned away to the dining-room and the front hall. It was nearly ten. He waited in front of the cuckoo clock until the little wooden door flew open and the wooden bird fell out, gasping the hour. Then he went on, still searching for a place to put his soldiers.

At the top of the stairs, in the narrow hall, Robert was confronted by the framed high school and college diplomas of Aunt Clara and Uncle Wilfred,

and the Morison coat of arms, and a picture of Grandfather Morison in his casket with all the funeral flowers. To the left were the Spare Room and Aunt Clara's
and Uncle Wilfred's bedroom, which looked as if it
were never slept in, though it was, every night. To the
right was Grandmother Morison's room. He stopped
at the door and looked in. Grandmother Morison was
in her rocking-chair by the window, and Bunny on
the big mahogany bed with a blanket thrown over
him. Neither one of them knew that Robert was there.
The room was littered with dress-patterns, quilting-
pieces, chalk, ribbon, old letters, spools, boxes and baskets and bags. *Come in if you're going to come in*,
she always said. *Or stay out if you're going to stay
out.* . . . He sniffed (there was a faint odor of camphor) and passed on down the hall to Uncle Wilfred's
study—a narrow dark little room with a cot and a
wardrobe and two chairs, a roll-top desk, a typewriter
table, and a place in the middle to walk among them.
The state agents of the Eureka Fire Insurance Company looked down at Robert from their oval frame,
and stared him out of countenance. The wallpaper
was brown and like a sickly sweet taste on his
tongue. But the wardrobe was exactly what he had
been looking for.

He put the soldiers on top of it, back and hidden
from sight. As he turned to go out of the room he was
stopped by the sound of a train whistle: two long, two
short, and then a mournful very long . . . Robert listened until he heard it again. Two long . . . two short
. . . And knew all in one miserable second that his fa-

ther and mother were on that train; that they had gone
away and left him in this house which was not a comfortable kind of house, with people who were not the
kind of people he liked; and that he would not see
them again for a long time, if ever.

9

Grandmother Morison could not remember the names
of people, or where she put things. "James," she would
say to Robert—"Morison—*Robert*," she would say;
"have you seen my glasses?" And they would be on
her forehead all the time.

When she had pulled them down, she would talk
to Robert in a comfortable way about the *Luisitania*,
or the assassination of President Garfield, or the Bom-
bardment of Fort Sumter. And about his Great-uncle
Martin, who owned a cotton plantation in Mississippi.
And how if the Southern people had only been nice
to the darkies and called them *mister* and *missus* there
would never have been any war. And about St. Paul.
And about Christ, who was immersed in spite of what
anybody said to the contrary, because he went down
under the water and he came up *out* of the water.

So long as Robert did not get up on the bed with
his shoes on, or ask questions when she was involved
in her crocheting, he could play with anything that

he liked. And by trial and error he discovered that Grandmother Morison's room was the one place in the house where he was safe. Everywhere else a voice said *Robert* the minute he touched anything. If he grew restless (as he invariably did) and wandered into the Spare Room, or downstairs, it was only a matter of time before he was impaled by Aunt Clara's voice saying *Robert, I thought I told you not to play with Uncle Wilfred's scrap-book. . . . That darning egg, Robert, belonged to your Great-grandmother Burnett. I don't believe I'd play catch with it, if I were you. . . . Robert, do you really think that's a nice kind of a song for you to be singing?* . . . Until he was afraid to do or say anything, so he sat in the front hall folding and unfolding his hands. Or stood with his nose to the front window, watching the children pass —running, sliding, pushing each other on the icy walks.

He knew all of them by name. The boys who dragged sleds after them, and the little girls who made angels in the snow. He knew what marbles some of the older boys had in their pockets. But if they looked up and saw him, there was no flash of recognition. Nothing but wonder, as though they were looking at a Chinaman. He was cut off from them, estranged. Their mothers had not gone to Decatur to have a baby.

When there was nothing out-of-doors to interest him, Robert would turn and wait for the cuckoo clock to strike. The wooden door flew open, and the noisy little bird fell out, and that restored his interest in living. Also it reminded him of how he let his mother into the room where Bunny was—a thing he would rather not have remembered. When he had managed to forget it again, he was still aware vaguely that there was something he *had* been worrying about.

One day became for him hopelessly like another. Even Thanksgiving, because Aunt Clara had roast chicken instead of turkey, which was sixty cents a pound. But on the Saturday after Thanksgiving he made a discovery; something that he had overlooked. Under the table in the living-room was an unabridged dictionary, and on top of it seven or eight other big books arranged according to size. He took them all off at once, in such a way that he could put them back again the instant he heard Aunt Clara coming.

Finding the wrong kinds of words in the dictionary was not a crime. They couldn't put him in jail for it. But it was a thing he would not want to be caught doing, especially by Aunt Clara. It was like telling lies or listening to people who didn't know he was there.

The best way was to pick a letter (like *C*), close his eyes, and turn to whatever page he came to: *chilblain . . . child . . . childbearing . . . childbed . . . childbirth . . .* He had gone past what he was looking for. "With child," people said. A woman was with *child (chīld) n.; pl. children (chĭl'drĕn) . . .* 1. *An unborn or recently born human being; fetus; infant; baby . . . A young person of either sex, esp. one between infancy and youth; hence, one who exhibits*

the characteristics of a very young person, as inno-
cence. . . .

Robert flushed. He looked around at the empty
chairs in the sitting-room and was on the verge of
closing the dictionary. Then he thought better of it.

obedience, trustfulness, limited understanding,
etc. . . . "When I was a child, I spake as a child, I
understood as a child. . . ." His skin felt warm, under
his clothing. He had gone too far again: fetus was the
word . . . *fetter . . . fettle, fettle . . . fettling . . .*
fetus, foetus (fē'tŭs), n. a bringing forth, brood, off-
spring, young ones; akin to L. fetus *fruitful, fructified,*
that which is or was filled with young . . . the young
or embryo of an animal in the womb. . . . Bunny
came up behind him, so quietly that Robert did not
even know he was in the room. Bunny waited a moment, and then made a slight noise. Robert slammed
the book together, in panic.

"If she catches you," Bunny said, "if she finds out
you've been using her dictionary, you'll get Hail
Columbia!"

"She won't find out."

"What'll you do if she does?"

"Nothing."

"Why are you so red in the face, then?"

"I'm not."

"You are, too."

"I'm not, either. For cryin' out loud, Bunny, go
play somewhere!"

"I will," Bunny said, hopefully, "if you'll let me
have your good soldiers?"

"Nothing doing."

The page was creased where Robert had been reading. He put it back carefully. It might be some time before Aunt Clara used the dictionary, and then she might not be looking for a word that began with C . . . *The young,* he read, *or embryo of an animal in the womb.* . . .

Bunny went out of the room, leaving Robert free to thumb through the *W*'s . . . *wolves* . . . *wolvish . . . woman . . . woman's rights . . . womb . . . The belly . . . The abdomen . . .* "*Transgressors from the womb*"—*Cowper . . . Any cavity like a womb in containing and enveloping.* . . . Robert read and reread, skipping the brackets and the abbreviations but with never a glimpse of the meaning. The meaning was there, but he could not get at it. It was inside the words.

What Robert wanted, suddenly, was to be outdoors in a vacant field, running. He wanted to be running hard, and with a football against his ribs; to be tackled and thrown on something hard like the ground. With a sigh, he closed the dictionary and put the other books on top of it. Then he went to the front door to see if the mail had come. It had, and there was a letter for Aunt Clara, in his father's handwriting. Robert took it to her and waited, with his heart pounding inside his shirt.

"It's from your father," she said, as she wiped her hands on the roller towel in the kitchen. "I say it's a letter from your father." She opened the letter and read it from beginning to end, slowly. When she had finished, she put it back in the envelope and the envelope in the pocket of her kitchen apron.

"Has the baby come?" Robert asked.

"No."

"Does he say how my mother is?"

"Your mother is fine—getting along as well as can be expected, he says."

Robert looked at her. "Is that all he says?"

"Yes, that's all. . . ."

But it wasn't, Robert assured himself on his way upstairs. He could tell by her eyes. There was something in that letter which Aunt Clara hadn't told him. He might go to the phone and call Dr. Macgregor, perhaps, and find out how things were. But his mother said not to bother him unless it was something important and this might not be.

But then again, Robert said to himself as he reached the head of the stairs, it might. He turned down the hall and saw at once that Bunny was trying to get at his soldiers. Bunny had pulled Uncle Wilfred's swivel-chair across the study and was teetering on it, in front of the wardrobe.

"Hey!"

Bunny turned a frightened face upon him and lost his balance. The soldiers fell with him, all the way to the floor.

"I didn't go to . . . really I didn't!"

Robert brushed past him without a word. There were his Cossacks with arms broken off, and heads, and rifles, and the legs of their white horses. His mouth twisted in pity. There were his lancers.

"Damn you," he said. "Damn you, Bunny . . .
Damn you!"

10

With glue and matches, wire, toothpicks, and pieces
of thread Robert worked over his broken soldiers all
Sunday morning. Fortunately the legs of certain
horses were all in one piece. He could make those legs
stay on. And if the horses wouldn't stand up afterward, he could always pretend that they were lame.
Arms could be fastened on with wire, and heads with
matches. So that anyone standing off at a distance
from them could hardly tell that the soldiers were
mended. The trouble was that Robert didn't play with
them standing off at a distance.

Bunny wanted to help, but Aunt Clara said no,
Robert didn't deserve any help after speaking to his
brother like that—which was all right with Robert.
When Bunny got big enough so that they were both
grown up and the same size, he was going to take
Bunny out in the back yard and clean up on him. That
might not put any soldiers back together again, he
told himself (and Bunny) but it would certainly make
him feel a lot better. Because every so often, with
the soldiers spread around him on the sitting-room
floor—an arm here and part of a sword or a helmet

there—he would suddenly decide it was too long a time to wait until Bunny grew up, and that something could be done right then and there. Uncle Wilfred was sitting in the big chair, with the Sunday paper, and so nothing was.

At five minutes to one, Aunt Clara called Robert and Bunny to come wash their hands for dinner. Bunny got to the kitchen sink first and took so long that it was time to sit down before Robert had his turn at the soap. He did not feel obliged, therefore, to wash with any great thoroughness or be too particular about not leaving any dirt on the roller towel. Besides, he said to himself as he sat down and unfolded his napkin, he was hungry.

At home it wasn't considered cheating if he started in on his salad before everyone else had been served. But no sooner did he commence than Aunt Clara spoke to him in a hushed voice.

"Robert, you've forgotten something."

He glanced up in surprise and saw that they were all looking at him—Aunt Clara, Uncle Wilfred, Grandmother Morison, and Bunny. He put down his salad fork and bowed his head. Uncle Wilfred in a disapproving voice said, "Bless us, O Lord, and these thy gifts. . . ."

Even after the blessing had been asked and they were free to receive it, Uncle Wilfred was not restored to a good humor. So far as Robert could make out, *he* was not responsible. It was the health officer, who had requested that for the duration of the epidemic the Christian Church (together with all the other churches) close its doors. To Uncle Wilfred's mind, there was no need for such action.

"It's one thing," he said, passing over the wing, which was Robert's favorite piece of chicken and giving him the drumstick, which he never ate if he could help it; "it is one thing to close the bowling-alley and the pool-halls. But to close the church of Jesus Christ is something else again. Anybody would think that church gatherings are unhealthy—that they're particularly conducive to the spread of disease."

Aunt Clara said, "It's true that there's lots of sickness about. I say that much is true."

"Church," Uncle Wilfred said, "is of so little importance that they can afford to suspend it at the slightest pretext. . . . There's no reason that I can see why people who come together for an hour on Sunday should be any more exposed to disease than they are all day long in stores and offices."

Robert was not hungry now. While Uncle Wilfred was talking, all desire for food left him.

"It's cold in here," he said, not expecting that Aunt Clara would get up and go look at the thermometer.

"I declare . . . seventy-six. Don't you feel well, Robert?"

He was all right. Perfectly. There was no reason why they should all be staring at him that way.

"Your eyes look bloodshot."

Robert pushed his chair back from the table. "No," he said, "I just thought it was cold in here."

And before he could get upstairs to the bathroom, he was vomiting.

Aunt Clara undressed him, as much as he would let her; and pulled the covers back so that he could get into bed. In a little while, Dr. Macgregor came and took his temperature and asked him questions—all from too great a distance to be of any help. Robert was glad that Dr. Macgregor had come, and sorry when he went away. But there was nothing that he could do about it. He was cut loose. He was adrift utterly in his own sickness.

For three days and three nights it was like that.

Aunt Clara appeared every two hours—now fully dressed, and now in a long white nightgown with her hair in braids down her back. Sometimes her coming was so slight an interruption that he could not be sure afterwards whether she had been there at all. Again she stood beside his bed for an indefinite time, with two white tablets in one hand and a glass of water in the other.

On the morning of the fourth day, Robert awoke from a sound sleep and knew that he was better. He knew also that there was something that he had to find out, as soon as he could remember what it was. Aunt Clara appeared with his breakfast tray.

"Good-morning," she said. "How do you feel? I say how are you feeling, Robert?"

"Better."

His voice sounded weak and like the voice of somebody else.

"I think I'll get up, Aunt Clara."

"You'll do no such thing. You've been a sick boy, Robert. A mighty sick . . ."

The letter . . . Quite suddenly it came to him. Aunt Clara got a letter and she wouldn't tell him what was in it. He was going to call Dr. Macgregor and find out how things were. And when Dr. Macgregor came, he was too sick to remember it.

"Aunt Clara, can you tell me how my mother is?"

"She's getting along about as well as can be expected, the doctor says. And she's in the hospital, where she'll get very good care."

Robert was not at all satisfied. As soon as she went out of the room, he turned his back to the wall, so that he would not have to look at the insurance agents, and slept. At noon Aunt Clara awakened him to give him his medicine. He asked her the same question and got a similar answer. He closed his eyes and slept and woke up again and slept again until he had disposed of the greater part of a winter afternoon. The street lamp shone in squares upon the ceiling. Turning then, Robert saw, distantly, as through the wrong end of opera glasses, things that had taken place a month before. The last Sunday in October they wedged themselves into the car, among fishing-poles, baskets of food, skillets, automobile robes, water-bottles, and the can of worms. Then they drove out into the country until they came to a special gate. After that they had to crawl through a barbed-wire fence and lug all they had brought with them to a clearing on the banks of a creek.

With the automobile robes spread out on the ground and the food put away, his father went far downstream to cast for pickerel and bass. His mother sat on a high bank where all the sunfish in the creek would come, sooner or later, to be caught by her. Bunny sat near her among the roots of an old tree, and let the fish nibble the bait off his hook while he was dreaming. And Robert went up the creek and over a bridge to a place where he could cast without getting his line caught in the overhanging branches.

His mother smiled at him foolishly from the opposite bank. And it seemed to him that she was smiling at the sky also, and at the creek, and at the yellow leaves which came down, sometimes by the dozen, and sailed in under the bank and out again.

II

When Robert awoke it was quite dark outside, and what Aunt Clara was saying downstairs came up to him distinctly through the register.

"Yes. . . . Yes, Amanda. . . ."

Her voice was pitched for the telephone.

"I'm pretty well. How are you? . . . I say I'm pretty well. . . . Yes . . . he's better, I think . . . I say Robert's better. Been asleep off and on most of the day. . . . Yes . . . in Decatur. . . . Yes . . . in spite of every precaution . . . both of them . . . James, too. . . ."

Robert sank back on the pillow. It was his mother and father that they were talking about. Something had happened to his mother and father while he was sick. Or before, maybe. And Aunt Clara wouldn't tell him. When she came up with his dinner he would say *How is my mother? You have to tell me.* . . . But that was not the way that things worked out. Before it was time for his tray, Robert heard the front-door bell ring, and Irene's voice in the downstairs hall. He sat up in bed feeling very dizzy and not altogether sure that what he heard was not imagined.

"I don't know, Irene . . ."

Aunt Clara was arguing with her.

"I say I don't know whether Robert ought to see anybody or not. He's still running a temperature and the doctor's orders are that——"

Robert could not bear it another second.

"Irene," he called, "I'm up here!"

He heard the sound of high heels upon the stair, and knew beyond all doubt that there was one person in the world who was not afraid of Aunt Clara.

Irene switched the light on. She was very beautiful as she stood in the doorway. Her eyes were shining and she was all in black, with a black fur around her neck. She came and sat down on the bed, beside him, and Robert could smell her perfume. That was a joke. Everything, suddenly, had become a joke. His hands (which she was holding) and the dun-colored wallpaper, the insurance agents. But most of all, the joke was on Robert himself—for being foolish enough to get sick at Aunt Clara's house.

"I've been to Chicago," Irene said, as if that too were foolishness.

So much had happened since she sat on the stairs with him. He did not ask why she had gone to Chicago. He did not care. When he was little and did something that he shouldn't—like turning the hose on Aunt Eth, who was starting out to the Friday Bridge Club—he set out for Irene's as fast as he could go. If he got there, he was safe. Irene would not let anybody come near him. Her eyes blazed and she put him behind her and said, *James Morison, don't you touch a hair of this child's head!"*

Robert looked at Irene carefully, trying to memorize her face and the buckle on her hat so that he would have something when she was gone. In her handkerchief there was a sponge soaked in face powder, like the one his mother carried. He listened with only a part of his mind to the story that she was telling—how she got lost on the street in Chicago.

". . . When I was sure that I didn't have the vaguest idea where I was, I went up to a policeman and said *Can you please tell me how to get back to the Palmer House?* And he said *Lady, follow your nose.*"

Robert smiled and spoke her name slowly.

"Irene . . ."

"What is it?"

"There's a girl who called here a little while ago. Her name is Amanda Matthews."

"Yes, Robert."

"They talked about my mother. . . . When I ask Aunt Clara how she is, Aunt Clara always says *getting along as well as can be expected*."

He could not frame the question that was troubling him, but Irene seemed to know anyway. She nodded to him just as if he had spoken it aloud.

"Turn over," she said. Then she pulled the covers down and rubbed his back the way she used to do when he was little—rubbed it until he felt drowsy and quiet, far inside of him.

"Your mother and father both have the flu, and they're very sick."

When he turned around to look at her, she was staring out of the window.

"Your mother has double pneumonia."

Robert turned his back to the wall and closed his eyes. He had found out now what it was that he wanted to know.

"The baby was born yesterday . . . is still alive. I talked to the doctor this noon. He said that your mother was slightly improved. . . . She has an even chance, he said."

12

After Irene had gone, Robert sought in his mind and in his fever for a way to describe the situation. He did not want to use certain words that frightened him.

Double pneumonia, Irene had said. And both his father and his mother were in the hospital.

And there was Aunt Amelia's husband, for instance. Mr. Shepherd had pneumonia (the plain kind) winter before last and there was something called *the crisis.* When that was over, he got well. But people didn't always.

Miss Harris at school didn't get well. She had "*T.B.*" and that was why she was so pale. She taught geography and all the kids used to bring her apples and oranges, and lilacs when they were in bloom. And for her birthday the whole class gave her sweet peas from the greenhouse.

When she had to stop teaching, Robert and Irish rode out to see her one afternoon on his bicycle. She was in a downstairs room, in bed, and she had changed so much during that short time that they hardly knew her. She coughed when she tried to talk to them. And there was a clock in the room that ticked loudly, and they were not allowed to stay but a minute or two.

That was several years ago. Before that Robert could remember about his Grandfather Blaney. Out in the country at a place called Gracelands they kept a ferret to drive the rats away. The ferret bit Grandfather Blaney in the ear while he was sleeping. Then he came home and was sick a long time, so that they had to have the Christmas tree upstairs in his bedroom. When the door was opened, Bunny and Agnes rushed in together—Agnes crying *See my rocking-horse,* and Bunny *Oh, see my doll!*

Then Grandfather Blaney died and the door of

his room was kept tightly closed. Robert opened it
once when there was nobody around, and went inside. They had taken everything out of the room except the furniture. There weren't even any clothes in
the clothes-closet.

When he went home, he talked to his mother
about it. She told him how they thought Grandfather
Blaney was dead, and how he opened his eyes and
looked at them and said, *Heaven is a providing-place.*
. . . That was very much like something Mr. Stark
read in Sunday school: *In my Father's house are many
mansions.* The same thing, practically. If people were
good, Mr. Stark said, and didn't break the Ten Com-
mandments, they went straight to Heaven when they
died. Cats and dogs, too. Only that wasn't right. Robert knew that for certain, because Irish's cat had kit-
tens that had to be killed. And he and Irish buried
one of them in a Mason jar with a little water in it.
And two weeks later they dug the jar up again.

There were some things it was better not to think
about. Without thinking at all, therefore, Robert lay
quietly while moment after moment rose over him
and set. Some one came upstairs. He heard the toilet
being flushed and the sound of water running in the
bathroom. Then there was no sound at all, until Uncle
Wilfred brought his dinner up to him.

He would have liked to talk about his mother,
but he didn't feel that he knew Uncle Wilfred well
enough. Uncle Wilfred was kind and all that. He
didn't force medicine down Robert's throat before he
was half awake. And when he turned the light on, he

always put a piece of paper around it. But on the other hand, Uncle Wilfred wasn't like other men. He didn't smoke or drink whisky or tell stories about how there were two Irishmen named Pat and Mike. He didn't have his hair cut often enough and he didn't believe in dancing. He wore shoes that turned up at the toe and he went to church three times on Sunday and there wasn't much of anything that Robert could talk to him about.

Each of them remained in a separate silence while Robert ate. But the moment Uncle Wilfred went out of the room, Robert was sorry that he had let Uncle Wilfred go, for he remembered, as soon as the light was turned out, that if anything happened to his mother, it would be *his* fault. He was frightened, then —more so than he had ever been. A terrible kind of fright, as if he were going to cry and be sick at his stomach, both at once. He doubled up his fists and buried his face in the hot pillow. The darkness was suffocating, but he stayed that way until he fell asleep, into a dream canopied with light.

He had come home.

He was in the little sewing-room at the head of the stairs.

It was night.

Waiting to go to sleep, he heard the stairs creaking.

And voices on the stairs.

The voices of his aunts, saying *Robert can't . . . Robert can't say . . . can't say fevver . . .* Aunt Clara, Aunt Eth, Irene. Their voices elongated in the dark and yet recognizable, saying the same thing one after another.

It made him uneasy. He turned, clutching the hem of his blanket.

Feather . . . Feather . . .

He could say it now without any trouble. Light as a . . . but not when he was little.

Feather . . .

The word snapped conclusively.

Feather . . .

It scraped against the dark side of the house and there was laughter on the stairs.

Feather . . .

The night wind bound him, dark, divided, on his hollow bed. Unwillingly, having premonitions of anguish, he settled farther into sleep.

In his dream he heard ringing, hoofs clopping, clopping on hard pavement. . . . He saw Dreyfus with his brown flanks shining. He heard Dreyfus with his harness jigging. . . . With faces white and intent Boyd and Irene drove past him in a high black carraige. He ran after them, crying *Irene! Irene!* but they did not hear him. And so he tried to climb on the back end of the carriage, crying

Irene!

(wildly)

As the wheels, turning

Do you hear me, Irene?

dragged him . . .

Torn bodily, torn by the roots out of his dream,

he sat up in the dark. Some one was shaking him.

Robert darling, wake up!

It was his mother.

I am awake.

You're not.

I am, too.

Then tell me what's the matter?

Sighing, he lay back upon the pillow. The bed-springs creaked under his dead weight. He was very tired.

I don't know . . . I was having a bad dream.

I heard you, clear in my room.

She bent over him in the dark and brushed the hair back from his forehead.

It must have been a very bad dream.

Yes, it was.

Sleep was still under him, like a pit.

He could look down. . . .

If his mother would only stay with him, he would not drop into it immediately and dream that same dream. But he could not ask her to do that. He was too old. Much too old.

It's this room, Robert.

She seemed to have guessed, anyway.

Without his having to tell her, she went to the window and adjusted the shade so that it wouldn't snap.

You're not used to sleeping in this room.

She came back then, and sat down beside him on the edge of the bed.

His head cleared.

His lungs were no longer expanding and contracting with excitement.

When he was quite calm inside, he started down. . . . He was not afraid now. His mother was there, and she was not going away just yet. There was no need to hurry.

Once he looked back, trying to say good-night to her, but no words came.

He had gone too far.

There was a great distance between them.

At the very bottom, he turned and saw that she was still sitting on the edge of the bed where he had left her.

13

Robert was not supposed to get up. Tomorrow, Dr. Macgregor said, if he didn't have any fever. But it was not hard. So long as Robert braced his arms against the side of the bed, he felt all right. It was only when he stood. Or when he bent over to pull on his stocking. He had to rest a little. And again before he could finish tying his shoe. Then he stood, one-legged and shivering, while he measured the distance across the room to the wardrobe where Aunt Clara had hung his suit. The floor tilted slightly—not any more than he had expected and not enough to make him fall. He drew on his underwear and his shirt. While he was adjusting the straps of his leg, a sparrow came to peck at a grain of paint on the window sill and Robert waved his arms weakly to frighten it away.

Before he had finished dressing, the telephone rang and Aunt Clara's voice came up through the register. Robert drew his belt on and buckled it, listening.

"Hello. . . . Hello, James, I can't hear you . . . I say I can't hear you very well. Can you hear me? . . . Yes. . . ."

At the thought of his father, Robert had to sit down and with both hands cling to the edge of the chair.

"You don't mean it, James. . . ." And then a long silence and, "No, but I will . . . if you want me to."

Straining, Robert heard the click of the receiver. The stairs creaked softly.

"Bunny . . . *Oh*, Bunny. . . ."

Aunt Clara was already at the head of the stairs when Robert pulled his door open. She was neither surprised to see him nor angry.

"Come in here, Robert," she said. "I have something to tell you."

He followed her into Grandmother Morison's room. Bunny was there alone. And he was in his pajamas. Aunt Clara sat down in the rocking-chair and gathered Bunny onto her lap.

"It's about your mother," she said.

Her voice sounded hoarse, as if she had a cold.

She began to rock back and forth, back and forth, until her eyes covered over with tears. Robert turned then and went out of the room.

He did not have to be told what had happened. He knew already. During the night while he was sleeping, she got worse. Then she did not have an even chance, like the doctor said. And she died. His mother was dead.

Book Three

UPON A COMPASS-POINT

I

If James Morison had come upon himself on the street, he would have thought *That poor fellow is done for.* . . . But he walked past the mirror in the front hall without seeing it and did not know how grey his face was, and how, all in a few days, sickness and suffering and grief and despair had aged him.

It was a shock to step across the threshold of the library and find everything unchanged. The chairs, the white bookcases, the rugs and curtains—even his pipe cleaners on the mantel behind the clock. He had

left them there before he went away. He crossed the
room and heard his own footsteps echoing. And
knew that, now that he was alone, he would go on
hearing them as long as he lived.

Sophie followed him when she had hung his coat
and hat in the hall closet. "There's some letters for
you," she said.

"Some what?"

"There's some letters for you and some bills.
They come while you were gone."

"Oh," James said.

"I put them on the table."

He looked at Sophie for the first time and saw
that her eyes were red from weeping.

"I thought I'd tell you," she said.

"Yes."

"In case there might be something important."

"Yes, I'll look at them"—he realized suddenly
why she looked so different. It was because she had no
teeth. And with her mouth sunken in, Sophie had
become an old woman—"after a while."

"I turned the spread back in your room so you
can lay down if you want to, Mr. Morison."

She saw that he didn't hear her and tried again.
"Mrs. Hiller telegraphed from Decatur yesterday.
She said to come and open the house this morning.
And have the guest-room ready for Miss Blaney."

"For Miss Blaney? . . . Oh yes, I forgot about
that. Or maybe they didn't tell me. It's all right,
though. When is she coming?"

"The telegram didn't say. It just said to have the

guest-room ready for her when she come. And Karl is going away."

"Where?"

"Why, didn't he tell you, Mr. Morison? He's going to Germany."

"Maybe he did. Yes, I guess so. When?"

"Right away. In a couple of days."

James put his hands over his eyes and felt the relief of darkness. His eyelids were cracked and hard. He had not slept for three nights. It did not seem likely that he would ever sleep again.

"You must tell Karl to be sure and see me before he goes."

Sophie nodded. "He was here early this morning. I had him build a fire in the grate. All you have to do is light a match to it."

"That's fine."

"When he comes I'll tell him you want to see him, Mr. Morison."

James took the stack of letters and sat down. *Mr. James B. Morison . . . Mr. James Morison, 553 W. Elm Street, Logan, Illinois . . . Mr. and Mrs. James B. Morison . . .* He read the envelopes again and again, without having the strength or the will to open them. *Mr. and Mrs. James B. Morison. . . .* When he closed his eyes for a moment and sank back, it was more than he could do to raise his head from the cushions.

"It's like being drunk," he said.

To his surprise, Sophie was still there and answered him.

"Once when I was a girl in the old country——"

James did not hear the end of her sentence. If he listened to Sophie, he would have to look at her. He would have to open his eyes.

When he relaxed, when he sat too long in one place, he invariably found himself on the railway platform downtown, with her. The train was coming in—the one they were going to take to Decatur. And there were people walking up and down the platform, waiting to get on. He shoved forward, knowing each time that if he'd only waited—but he didn't wait. That was the whole trouble. He was trying to get seats for the two of them before all the others got on. If he'd stepped back, he'd have seen the interurban draw up alongside the train. On the other tracks . . . The interurban had a parlor car that was almost empty. It would have been ever so much better to take that, don't you see? And turn their train tickets in later. That way they wouldn't have been exposed. But they had suitcases and all the people were pushing them forward and the train was crowded already. There was nothing to do but go up the steps and onto the train.

"You must take care of yourself, Mr. Morison," Sophie said. "You've got those three young children to think about. If anything happened to you now——"

"Yes," James said, "you're quite right." And sprang up suddenly and began tearing the envelopes open, one after another. He read the letters while he walked back and forth between the fireplace and the windows—read them over and over without retaining what he read. Then he threw envelopes and letters upon the library table and stood perfectly still, pressing his shoulder against the mantel.

For two days now (ever since they came into his room at daybreak to tell him) he had been getting on that train. And there was no way, apparently, that he could stop.

2

The coffin was set in the bay window of the living-room, and James wanted to be alone, but almost as soon as the undertaker's men were out of the house, Wilfred appeared, bringing James's mother and Bunny.

Bunny was weeping.

James bent down and drew Bunny to him, be-tween his knees, and felt the soft wet cold cheek against his own rough skin.

"There, there," he said, gently. "You mustn't, son. You mustn't take on so. You'll be sick." He strug-gled with the large buttons on the child's coat.

"I put his rubbers on," Wilfred said.

James looked at him earnestly.

"I say I put Bunny's rubbers on."

"Oh . . . much obliged to you."

"That's all right," Wilfred said. "Glad to do it, only I think I got them wrong foot to."

James nodded. If they'd only wait, let him be by himself for a while.

"Clara said to tell you she'd be over this evening right after supper."

"You must take your coats off," James said. "You mustn't stand here in the front hall." And wondered if his words sounded as desperate to them—and as foolish.

His mother unwound a heavy woolen scarf and looked at him with faded eyes.

"James," she said solemnly, "she is gone to a better place, where she'll always be happy. Fourteen years ago your father died—in March. And it doesn't seem like any time at all. . . ."

Neither does what happened night before last, James wanted to say to her. He was only two rooms down the hall at the hospital, and Thursday night, when she was worse, he lay awake all night, listening. The gas-light came through the transom and cut a rectangular hole in the ceiling. It was through that hole that the sound of her desperate suffocated breathing came to him.

"You don't know, I said to Clara, how many times I get down on my knees and thank God for taking him, for not letting him suffer." She allowed Wilfred to help with her coat. "Every few days he'd have a spell of very bad pain. Then we'd have to give him morphine. . . ."

When Bunny stopped weeping and turned to look at her, James separated him from his coat and mittens.

"Sophie is out in the kitchen," he said. "Why don't you go out and say hello to her."

There was no point in a child's knowing these things.

"I'd been waiting for him to go," his mother said as they went into the library. "I'd been expecting it ever since he stopped eating. That's what carried him along, the doctor said—a good appetite. And he'd lost so much flesh. . . ."

With his eyes James begged Wilfred to take her away, but Wilfred was unable or unwilling. He sat down in the largest chair and crossed one knee over the other permanently.

"I don't think your father weighed much over a hundred and twenty or maybe a hundred and twenty-five, because there was nothing to him but skin and bones. Even so"—she turned and looked into Wilfred's face to make sure that he was listening—"even so, I didn't get much rest. It was hard lifting him, you know, and I stayed right in the same room with him for months. He'd rather lie there and suffer than call anybody. And I knew if I was near I'd hear him move. He'd have pain, you know, James. And then he'd take medicine and sleep."

There was a silence. James said, "Did you have a nice time in Vandalia, Wilfred?"

"In Vandalia? Why, we didn't go."

"I thought you and Clara were going down there for Thanksgiving."

"We did intend to. But we'd have had to go on the train, and with so much sickness about, we were afraid to risk it. But I thought Clara told you all that when you called up about the boys?"

"Yes, I guess she did. Have they been all right? And behaved themselves?"

"Robert's been sick."

"Oh . . . is that so?"

"Yes, Robert's been a sick boy," his mother said. "A mighty sick boy!"

"The flu?"

She nodded.

"Yesterday morning," Wilfred said, "after you called, Robert got up out of bed before he was supposed to. Today, the doctor said. But Clara got in touch with him during the forenoon and he said it was all right if Robert didn't have any temperature. And he didn't—this was yesterday—so I guess it *will* be. He has to keep quiet, of course."

James caught a glimpse of a pocket knife: Wilfred was going to pare his finger nails.

"He didn't seem to take it as hard as Bunny did. But then I always thought Bunny showed his mother more affection." Wilfred closed the knife blade with a sigh. "Clara was going to tell you but in case she forgets—if you want to bring the baby home after the funeral, we'd be only too glad to take it and look after it for you."

James sat up. "I don't know." He steadied himself carefully with his hands. "They're going to keep the baby at the hospital for a week or so. The baby's all right, I guess, but they want to keep it there. And after that I don't know exactly what I want to do. I haven't had time to think about it."

The front door opened while James was speaking.

"We want to be of help," Wilfred said, "in any way that we possibly can."

"That's very kind of you."

"Until you get straightened around," Wilfred said.

Irene appeared in a draft of cold air. Her coat was half unbuttoned. She spoke to each of them. Then gravely, without any expression on her face, she made her way around Wilfred's feet and drew the curtains together across the library windows. With grateful eyes James followed her. She turned on the table lamp, and in the blue bowl on the mantel found matches to light the fire. When Bunny came in, the room was bright and habitable.

She smiled at him. "You know your agate?" she said, and took the blue bowl down from the mantel. "The yellow agate that you told me was lost? Well I've found it."

Bunny went on looking at her face.

"Here it is."

"Irene," Bunny said, "it's so terrible here!" And buried his face in the lining of her coat.

Irene's smile went all to pieces. She knelt down and put her arms about him. "Everything's going to be all right," she said. "Only you mustn't cry, do you hear? You mustn't cry."

Bunny dried his face with the back of his hand, and took the bowl and the yellow agate.

"I know," he said, and sat down on the floor to play.

Irene stood looking at him thoughtfully, until her eyes were no longer blurred. Then she turned to James and said, "When's Robert coming home?"

"He isn't, I guess."

"Why not?"

"He's been sick."

"I know he has. I just came from there."

"Clara doesn't think Robert ought to come home," Wilfred began. "He wasn't even supposed to——"

Irene interrupted him. "I called Dr. Macgregor and he said he'd seen Robert early this morning, and that it was all right if we wanted to bring him home. . . . Clara wouldn't listen, James. I told her . . . I told her everything Dr. Macgregor said. But she said Robert was going to stay there just the same. . . . I left him sitting in a chair by the front window with his rubbers on."

"If Clara doesn't think he ought to come home," James said, "perhaps it would be just as well to——"

"Don't you *want* him here?"

"Certainly I want him."

"Well do you mind if I call and tell her that?"

James shut his eyes. "Tell her anything you like."

He would have shut his mind, too, if it had been possible. He was very tired. And weak. And there was

no reason why they could not make these arrange-
ments among themselves.

From what Wilfred was saying—a word now and
then, or a phrase—James gathered that the churches
had been closed on account of the epidemic, but they
were soon to be opened again. As for the epidemic,
Wilfred said, that was on the wane. No new cases
had been reported yesterday or the day before.

Against his will James listened and heard Irene's
voice locked in argument.

"I know, Clara, but the doctor says it's all right
. . . yes. . . . Yes, James wants him here. . . ."

They had traced the epidemic, Wilfred said, to
the original source and found that it was brought to
this country in German submarines.

"Yes. . . . Yes, Clara. . . . Yes, I know!"

James turned and looked at Irene uneasily. There
was no color in her face.

"Yes," she said, very slowly. "Yes . . . yes . . ."

The brilliant unreasonable laughter shocked them
all and furthermore it didn't stop when it should have,
but went on and on into the mouthpiece of the telephone.

3

It was Wilfred who took the receiver out of Irene's
hand and told Clara to have the boy ready in fifteen
minutes. For that James would be grateful always.

Ethel came in from the late afternoon train and went upstairs right away to look after Irene. When his mother and Wilfred had gone, James stood with his back to the fire until the little brass clock on the mantel tick-tick-tick-ticked itself out of existence and the room grew quiet around him.

At five-thirty Robert came in. He had a book under one arm and the box of soldiers under the other, and he limped more noticeably than usual. When Robert was tired, he did not care how he walked, but led with his good leg, in spite of all that James had told him, and dragged his artificial leg behind.

Robert shook hands with his father solemnly and put the soldiers and the book on the library table. Then he went over to the windows and sat down.

"How are you feeling, son?"

"All right," Robert said.

"Weak?"

"Yes."

"So am I. We'll have to be careful for a while. Both of us."

Their eyes met and they agreed that there was something in the house which was not to be talked about. The best and possibly the only solution, so far as James could see, was for Clara to take the baby. And the boys, too. For he couldn't keep the house going—that was certain. He'd have to store what furniture he wanted. That wasn't much. He had never cared for antiques the way Elizabeth did. And sell all the rest. Sell the house, too, for what he could get.

Wilfred had not offered to take the boys, but it

would be all right, probably. James would give Clara so much a month for boarding them and for their clothes—because he would not have Wilfred or anybody else paying for the support of his children. And he'd get a room near by. Clara's wasn't the kind of home they were used to, perhaps. But it would do until such time as he was able to make a better arrangement.

In the long run it was a mistake to have children. James did not understand them. He never knew what was going on in their minds. But that was Elizabeth's doing, after all. It was she who had wanted them.

There were some men who had a natural way with children. Tom Macgregor, for instance. They came to him in a room full of people, and pestered the life out of him. When Bunny and Robert were little, they would come to their father sometimes to have cigar smoke blown into their ears—Bunny did still— when they had the earache. But not very often. If they had been girls it might have been different. James felt more at ease with little girls. They came and sat on his lap and played with his watch-fob. And they seemed to like very much the riddles he told them. Robert and Bunny were forever arguing, contending with each other like Cain and Abel. So that it was mostly a matter of keeping them separated and making each one play with his own toys. And without her . . . James went into the front hall and stared for a long time at the umbrella-stand. Without Elizabeth it was more than he could manage.

On the second trip into the front hall he went

through the white columns and into the living-room. Then into the library by the door at the farther end. If he could only go back, if he could remember everything during the last ten days, why then he might—it was foolish of course, but the same idea occurred to him over and over—he might be able to change what had already happened.

In his whole life he had never been sick before—not seriously. And being sick, he could not make people do the things he wanted them to. They would not even let him get up and go into her room at the hospital and see her—except that once, late Wednesday afternoon.

The nurse brought a chair for him and made him sit some distance away from the bed. Elizabeth was better, she said. But he could not help seeing how difficult it was for her to breathe. It seemed to take all her strength for that.

He looked at her hair spread out over the pillow, and remembered the first time he had ever seen her. She was driving a pony cart on Tremont Street and she had two little girls in the cart with her and the little girls wore big blue hair-ribbons.

He leaned forward to ask her if she remembered meeting him that day on Tremont Street, but just then the nurse came in. The nurse had the baby with her, wrapped in a white blanket. And Elizabeth smiled her slow smile and said, *Look, James, another peeing boy. . . .*

4

Each time that James passed through the living-room he was careful to look at the sofa or the French windows which led into the back part of the house. Nevertheless, he was drawn, pulled toward the bay window, until at last he could get no farther. The coffin was grey with silver handles. And if it was really Elizabeth, James thought—if he should see *her* when he stepped up to it (her dark hair and her forehead and the slope of her throat)—he did not know what he would do.

He stood there a few feet away, with his heart racing wildly like a machine, and Sophie had to call him twice to dinner before he understood.

Ethel and the boys were waiting for him in the dining-room.

"Would you like me to serve, James?" she said.

James looked at her in bewilderment. She pronounced her words precisely the way a school-teacher would.

"I always do the serving," he said.

"Yes, but I thought that perhaps if you weren't feeling well——"

"I'm all right," James said. "I'm quite all right."

They sat down together—Ethel in Elizabeth's place at the end of the table. When James was with her he found himself on guard for fear that he would make some mistake in his English. He spoke as well as the average person, he supposed. As well as anyone ought to speak. But Ethel had gone East to school. She had gone to Bryn Mawr and she never seemed to want to marry. When she was younger and before her hair turned grey, she was attractive enough. James knew of several men that she could have had. But she was too well educated for a woman and she didn't want any of them.

"For Miss Blaney," he said. And when Sophie took the plate that he handed her, James noticed that she was self-conscious on account of her mouth.

"How much are they going to cost, Sophie?" he said when she returned to his end of the table.

"What, Mr. Morison?"

"Your teeth."

"I don't know, exactly," she said, with the color mounting upward into her face. "About fifty dollars." She set Bunny's plate in front of him. "But if I'd known how much it would take, I don't guess I'd of had them out. But they were hurting me so, night and day——"

"You did the right thing, I'm sure," Ethel said. "And Robert needs more water."

James wondered if he had said something that he shouldn't have, if he had said something unkind. "When the time comes to get your new teeth, let me know, Sophie. I might be able to help you with them." He took up the carving-knife and began sharpening it.

And Sophie beside him pulled the hem out of her apron in an access of gratitude.

When Robert had been served, she returned once more to the head of the table.

"That Karl is here . . ."

James unfolded his napkin.

"Tell him I'll be out as soon as we're through dinner," he said.

Sophie disappeared through the swinging doors, and James took up his knife and fork. When he tried to eat, the food turned solid in his throat and would not go down. There was nothing to do but sit with his plate untouched before him, and watch his sons, who were still too young to confuse grief with a good appetite.

When Robert passed things it was always without speaking and without looking up—as if the interruption were barely tolerable. With Bunny it seemed to be largely a matter of making him hear, for he ate with his eyes on some object (the corner of a dish now) and there was no telling where his mind was.

"How is Irene?" James said.

"Resting. I put cold cloths on her head. That's about all anybody can do, you know, after she's had one of those spells."

When Ethel was a little girl, Elizabeth had said, she could not bear to get dirt on her clean white stockings.

Bunny was recalled from wherever it was that he had been.

"Is it true, Aunt Eth— Is it true that Irene married Uncle Boyd Hiller for his money?"

In the silence that followed this question they could all hear the big clock ticking sullenly in the front hall, two rooms away.

"No, son, it isn't true," James said. "And you mustn't say things like that, do you hear?"

Bunny nodded, and would have gone on eating if Ethel had not leaned forward in her chair with hard bright eyes.

"Who told you that, Bunny?"

"It's something he's made up," James said.

I didn't either make it up—it's what Grandmother Morison told Amanda Matthews."

Robert put his fork down with a clatter.

"Who is Amanda Matthews?" Ethel asked.

"She's a girl in Aunt Clara's Sunday-school class that was at Aunt Clara's house night before last."

James saw that Ethel was smiling at him queerly.

"Well, however it was," she said, "you misunderstood. Your grandmother wouldn't say such a thing."

"But she did, Aunt Eth. She said there was somebody else that Irene wanted to marry but Grandmother Blaney kept after her night and day, saying what a fine young man Uncle Boyd was, because he had been to Princeton and——"

"Bunny, that's enough."

The interurban was drawing alongside the train, on the other tracks. And James had to wait for a minute before he could go on speaking.

"Suppose you tell us, son, what you were doing all this time?"

"He was on the couch," Robert volunteered, "in the sitting-room, pretending like he was asleep."

"When I want information from you, Robert, I'll ask for it. . . . Go up to your room now, both of you."

They had made trouble enough for one evening —trouble that would last for months and months, and when Irene found out about it, breed more and more trouble.

"Well," he said, "what are you waiting for?"

As soon as they had gone—Robert looking injured and Bunny in tears again—James set about to deal with the image that obsessed him. With so much sickness, with the epidemic everywhere, it stood to reason that someone with influenza might have been on that interurban, too. They might have been exposed to the flu there, just as they were on the crowded train. And what point was there in torturing himself like this? What good did it do?

"You might have let them stay and have their dessert," Ethel said, from the other end of the table.

"They're my children, Ethel," James said, "and I'll do with them as I think best."

5

Wilfred returned with Clara almost immediately after dinner.

"It doesn't seem possible," Clara said. "I say it just doesn't seem possible! She was so young, and with so much to live for!"

James had no idea what to say, or what was expected of him. But as the evening progressed, more and more people came—Lyman and Amelia Shepherd, Maud Ahrens, the Hinkleys, the McIntyres, the Lloyds—until the library was filled with them. And by that time James had adjusted his mind to the rhetoric of the occasion. What bewildered him was not the set phrases, and not the repetition, but the fact that they were sincerely spoken. *Such a loss,* people said to him with tears in their eyes. *So tragic that she should have to be taken.* . . . Then because there were so many that they could not all talk to him, they fell back upon one another politely, as if that were why they had come. They discussed the peace terms and the price of meat. They talked about the weather, which was severe for December—only the beginning of the cold months.

James tried to take a suitable interest in the conversation, but he could not keep from glancing up when each new person came into the room, and strange ideas ran through his head. It seemed to him that except for an unwillingness to interrupt one another, people acted very much as if they had come here to a party. The house had taken possession of them—Elizabeth's house—and they were having a good time.

Clara and Wilfred went home, and then the Shepherds, and then the McIntyres, almost without James's noticing it. The air grew heavy with smoke. And after a while he discovered that it was not necessary for him even to seem to be listening. He was glad when eleven o'clock came and one by one they stood up to leave—all except young Johnston, who had brought his mail out to him from the office and did not know apparently how to go home.

While Johnston talked about the office and about the adjustment of a certain loss, James sat with his hand over his left side. It was something that he had never thought about until now, and there was no reason why it should occur to him particularly, except that he felt very wide awake after not having slept for days and days. But the strange thing was that he could hear his own heart ticking under his vest—keeping time there like a clock.

"I've come down from Chicago," a voice said—an unmistakable voice. James sprang up and went to the front hall, but he was too late. Boyd Hiller was there. He was inside the door, talking to Ethel, and there was that same tired handsomeness about him. He had not changed, except that it seemed to be an effort for him to carry himself so well. As Ethel started up the stairs, he turned and saw James in the doorway.

"Good evening," he said.

Once upon a time James met Boyd Hiller with Robert unconscious in his arms. And later (years later) James had shut the front door in his face. The extreme courtesy of Boyd's manner implied that he remembered both incidents.

In any family, James thought, it was like that. Nothing was ever forgotten.

There were no chairs in the front hall—only a sofa beside the window. Both men remained standing. When the tension became uncomfortable, James said, "Are you living in Chicago now?"

"For a short while."

Boyd cleared his throat.

"New York is my headquarters, though, and has been the last two years. I'm on the stock exchange."

"That must be interesting," James said, and thought grimly of the time Boyd put soap in the minnow-bucket for a joke.

"You get used to it."

"Yes, I suppose."

Irene was coming down the stairs in a green flowered kimono.

"You get used to anything," James said.

When Irene reached the bottom step, she waited, and Boyd waited at the edge of the dark red rug. "I can't tell you how shocked and how sorry I am!"

Irene stepped down and shook hands with him gravely.

"You've been sick," she said.

Boyd nodded.

"Flu?"

"It was a light case. When I was able to go back to the hotel I found your note, and here I am."

James understood now what had happened— why Irene had gone off to Chicago when they were counting on her to stay and look after the boys. Actually, there had never been much doubt in his mind. He knew her almost as well as he knew Elizabeth. She was very impulsive by nature, and excitable, and decided everything on the spur of the moment, and then had all the rest of her life to regret it in. It didn't take any great intelligence to see by the look on her face that she was about to run through that whole unhappy business with Boyd Hiller all over again. If they wanted to do that, James thought, it was all right with him. He turned and went back into the library.

6

The flowers in Irene's kimono were almost but not quite the color of her hair. And James decided that no matter what people said, it was not money. Irene had not married Boyd for that, nor would she go back to him for any such reason. There was no telling how she felt about Boyd now, but at one time, before they began quarreling so, she had been fond of him. On her wedding day she broke a mirror and perhaps it was that which ruined their marriage—bad luck as much as anything.

Somehow it was impossible to think of her leading a calm, ordinary life. Wherever Irene was, there was excitement. Now when she gathered the folds of her kimono and leaned toward the fire, her eyes glittered. Her hair gave off light.

"I think we know sometimes what is going to happen to us," she said. "I remember things that didn't seem to have any meaning till now, and they fit. . . . We were upstairs, James, in your bedroom, and Elizabeth was doing her hair. I was sitting on the bed, watching her, and I said, 'It's so complicated, the way you are doing your hair now,' and she stopped and looked at me in the mirror, and said, 'I know. I was just thinking that nobody will be able to do it for me when I am dead.' I said for her not to talk like that, because it was wrong and silly and there was no telling how long anybody would live. But she took the hairpins out of her mouth and said, 'Within three years.' "

James got up out of his chair and began to walk. He could not and would not believe what Irene was saying. He could not believe that Elizabeth had lain awake at his side, planning and arranging things for a time when she would not be there. With other people she sometimes covered up her true feelings, though not with him. Nobody had any idea, for instance, how deeply she still felt about Robert's accident; how at night she turned into his arms and wept. But if her life had been overshadowed by the anticipation of dying, he would have known it. She could not have kept it from him.

"It's the kind of thing that people remember," he said, "after some one is dead. You might never have thought anything more about it except for that. It's like any common superstition—thirteen at the table or a dog howling or a bird in the house."

"You know there was one," Irene said. "There was a bird in Bunny's room while he was sick. I didn't tell you afterward because I knew it would worry you— Not the bird, but something that it was too late to do anything about. It was my fault, really. Elizabeth sent Robert for a broom. Then in our excitement we both forgot and went into the room where Bunny was. When Robert came back he saw her sitting on the edge of Bunny's bed. . . . And ever since, he's been thinking that if anything happened to his mother, he'd be responsible. You didn't know that, did you, James? . . . Tonight when they were both in bed I went to see them. I talked to them for a while about their mother, and to my surprise Robert broke down and told me what was on his mind. You have to watch him, James, and talk to him more than you do, and find out what is back of what he's saying. Because he's at the age to get notions. . . . I explained to him that people caught the flu within three days after they were exposed to it. What he was worrying about happened weeks before his mother took sick. I don't know whether he believed me or not. I guess he did.

It's things like that—don't you see? Now that his mother isn't here to keep an eye on him . . . And each of us has his private nightmare. Robert isn't the only one."

James looked at her oddly to see whether by some mischance she knew about the interurban.

"I keep remembering," she said, "how selfish I was those last weeks—always thinking about Boyd and whether I could bring myself to go back to him. And I sort of took what was happening to her for granted. That was the way it always was. As a person, James, I could never hold a candle to her. Nobody could. . . . I remember once we went, the two of us, to see a woman who had cooked for my mother, and who was very sick. She lived in an old house on Tenth Street, and it was filthy dirty. And after we left, Bess was furious with me. She said 'Irene, I *saw* you gather up your skirts so they wouldn't touch anything! How *can* you be like that?' . . . She went over to the bed where the woman lay, and sat down, and took her hand."

James sighed. He had been along with them that day. It was just after Elizabeth and he were married. He had gone into the dirty ramshackle house on Tenth Street when they did. But Irene didn't remember. She was talking about Elizabeth for the pain it caused her, and possibly to keep from saying something she couldn't bring herself to say. They had always been friends, and with friends you oughtn't to have to say what both of you understand without its being said. Probably this was as near as she could come to speaking about that abrupt change of plans that had thrown them all into such an uproar. If it hadn't been for Clara, who, with all her faults, and she had plenty of them, nevertheless . . .

"And there's something else, James . . . something I have to tell you. At the last when she was so terribly sick she motioned with her hand. As if she wanted to write. I said 'Tell me what it is you want done, Bess, and I'll do it . . .'"

James got up and went to the window and threw it wide open, and small white papers that he had stuffed into the cracks to keep the drafts out were scattered across the room.

" 'It's about my baby,' she said. 'I don't want the Morisons to have my baby.'"

The air was not as cold as James had expected, but dark and full of snow.

7

When he opened the door from the butler's pantry into the kitchen, he found only darkness. It was no more than reasonable, he told himself, that Karl should have got tired waiting and gone home. For it was after eleven, and he had promised to come out as soon as dinner was over.

The scene at the table had driven everything else out of his mind. And people began coming. . . .

There was no need to say that to Ethel. She was a fine woman and he was fond of her. But if there was one thing that he could not stand, it was having somebody step in and tell him how to run his affairs. . . . He groped his way past the table to the light cord. Sophie had left the kitchen just as she always did, in perfect order. He was about to turn and go back to the front part of the house when he heard a scratching sound outside, and as he opened the door, there were two eyes shining at him out of the darkness. Old John hobbled across the sill.

"Did they forget you, old fellow?" James said.

The dog looked at him reproachfully.

It was beginning, James thought to himself—the final and complete disintegration of his house. Wherever he turned he would find it. Elizabeth was gone, and things would not be done which should be done. . . . He put his face down and buried it (for there was no one here to see him) in the cold fur of the dog's side. Old John whined softly.

Why, James thought, why am I doing this? And straightened up immediately and stood there waiting until the dog had made himself comfortable beside the stove. Then he turned the light out and went back the way he had come—through the butler's pantry and the dining-room and around the library to the front hall. Mr. Koenig had come over from next door, and he was in the library alone. And on the fifth step of the stairs James paused, remembering why people sat up all night with the dead.

Then he went on up the stairs and across the upstairs hall to the bedroom which Elizabeth and he had shared, and saw her dresses hanging in the closet, and was struck blind and almost senseless. When he could, he shut the closet door quickly, and pressed his forehead into the long cool mirror which was on the other side.

Satin
and lace
and brown velvet
and the faint odor of violets.

—That was all which was left to him of his love. In anger then (for she could have sent some word to him and she had not—only that message about the baby, which he didn't entirely believe) he went about the room picking up her brush or her ivory mirror or the tiny bottle of smelling-salts, and putting them down again. One after another he opened drawers, gathering small intimate things—hairpins, sachet-bags, a sponge soaked in powder, a score-card, a tassel, a string of amber beads—and made a pile of them on the dresser. For she had put him aside, he said to himself, casually with her life.

He stood in the center of the room, rocking forward and back; and in his ears heard that terrible last hour of her breathing. . . . He would sell the house, he thought over and over like a lesson to be memorized. A lesson that he would recite tomorrow when the time came. And Clara could take the children since she wanted them. And everything else—Elizabeth's clothes, her amethysts and pearls (he dumped them out on the dresser), her engagement ring, her enam-

eled watch—he would give to Ethel, to Irene, to
Sophie, to anybody with the kindness and mercy to
have them. Because she was gone now. And when he
had finished, there would be no trace of her anywhere.
No one would know there had ever been such a person, he said to himself. And turned to the doorway,
and saw Bunny staring at him with Elizabeth's frightened eyes.

8

When he had given Bunny a drink of water and
tucked him in bed, James went downstairs and out of
the house. The wind had fallen. There was an inch of
snow on the front walk and more of it coming down
steadily on James's coat sleeve and on his gloved hands
and whirling in a silent frenzy about the street lamp.
The crotches of trees were white with it, and each
separate branch outlined. When James looked up he
could see the night sky all dark, and the moist snow
dropping into his face, into his open mouth.

He had come down the stairs and out of the house
as he had done every day of his life, but with this difference—he was not going back. He would not
enter that empty house again. Here on the sidewalk
(with snow falling so thick that a man ten feet away
would hardly know him) he was alone.

He turned to the left, as the snow turned, and

walked past the first house, which was the Koenigs', and past the second, which was the Mitchells', and the third. . . . They were all asleep in their beds, with no knowledge of him, or that he was here on the sidewalk looking at their darkened houses.

The house of Elizabeth's father was on the other side of the street and occupied by strangers. He had nothing to fear from it. . . . He and Elizabeth lived there when they were first married, with her father and mother and with Irene. Elizabeth's father read Ingersoll and questioned every accepted idea on religion and morality, so that it was an education for a young man to be with him. But during his last illness he changed his mind about things, and he stopped questioning. *It's like this, James,* he would say. *There's the earth—the continents and the seas, and the moon revolving around the earth, and the sun beyond that, and all the constellations. And beyond the constellations are stars without number or name, millions of them, whirling in space. You know that, James, without my telling you.* . . . But for time or the passage of time they might be there now, talking—James himself, only younger, and an old man dying of a horrible blood infection in his head.

James leaned against a tree. The snow was all about him like a curtain. And he could almost believe that they were still in that house across the street. *Somebody made it—some power—according to laws that can't be changed or added to.* . . . *The same now as they were thousands of years ago.* . . . *It's got to be like that. Otherwise it wouldn't work.* . . .

When James put both hands behind him, he felt the rough bark of the tree through his leather gloves. His fingers were getting cold and stiff.

"But to what purpose?" he said aloud, and hearing the words, he lost their meaning and all connection with what had gone before.

He knew only that there was frozen ground under his feet, and that the trees he saw were real and he could by moving out of his path touch them. The snow dropping out of the sky did not turn when he turned or make any concession to his needs, but only to his existence. The snow fell on his shoulders and on the brim of his hat and it stayed there and melted. He was real. That was all he knew.

He was here in this night, walking across the corner of a yard, over a sidewalk, down a vacant street. When he stopped to get his bearings, he saw that without knowing it he had turned up the alley. There were deep frozen ruts along each side of the road, and telephone poles one after another leaning against the sky. Ahead of him he heard wheels creaking and the placing (muffled and delicate) of hoofs. The placing of hoofs on snow. And knew suddenly that it was all a mistake . . . everything that he had thought and done this day.

He was alive, that was the trouble. He was caught up in his own living and breathing and there was no way possible for him to get out. Elizabeth knew that, and she had come after him in the pony cart. She had come to take him home.

He was glad. He was immensely excited. His

hands shook and his knees. He began to run along the alley, stumbling and falling and picking himself up again. He ran until he was stopped by the lean shape of a horse, and a wagon with a lantern on it. The lantern shone upward into a man's face that was thin and patient and crazy.

With the last of his strength gone out of him, James leaned against the firm lattice-work of his own back fence.

9

James awoke late into a room that was bright with the morning sun. On the dresser were Elizabeth's things lying in a heap as he had left them. When he looked outside the snow blinded him. He stretched his legs under the covers until they touched the foot of the bed, and wondered how many mornings of his life he had lain here—awake and watching the curtains blow in from the open window. And whether the lightness he felt inside him was grief. Or if he would ever be capable of any emotion again.

Slowly and with care he bathed and shaved and dressed himself in clean clothes. He staggered slightly when he went from the closet to the dresser to comb his hair. But his head was clear, and when he put his hands to his eyelids, they no longer felt cracked and hard. . . . There were formalities and customs, there was the funeral to be got through with somehow this day.

Ethel was in the guest-room, making her bed. He lingered at the door until she noticed him.

"You look rested, James," she said. "Did you sleep?"

He looked into her eyes and saw nothing but kindness there—kindness and a veiled sympathy. It had never been easy for her to express her feelings.

"Yes, I think I did."

"That's what you needed more than anything else."

For the first time it occurred to him that Ethel might keep from Irene what Bunny said last night at the table—that she had, in fact, no intention of telling her.

"Thank you," he said, and hoped that she would understand what for.

"Irene is off on some errand. With Boyd, I think. But your mother is here and Clara, too. You'll find them in the sewing-room."

At the head of the stairs James listened and heard their voices. They were arguing over which card had come with which flowers.

"I don't care what you say, Clara, the yellow roses were from the men in James's office. The carnations were from Bunny's class at school."

"If you'd only waited, Mother, and let me open them. I'm trying to write them down in this little book as they come. Otherwise we'll never know who sent what."

Though it was nearly ten o'clock, there was no one in the front hall or the living-room or the library. And James's place was still set at the dining-room table. He went on to the kitchen, which was warm and bright. Karl sat with his overcoat on and the sweat running down his face. Bunny was beside him at the kitchen table. And Sophie, rattling the breakfast dishes, created such a cheerful noise that none of them heard James, or knew that he was there.

Bunny was making a wreath of ferns. And it was hardly the thing, James thought. Bunny ought not to be making a game of flowers that had been sent to his mother's funeral. As James started forward he could have sworn, almost, that he felt a slight restraining pressure on his arm. And he turned, in spite of himself —in spite of the fact that he knew positively no one was there.

10

With his coffee James smoked a cigarette—the first since he had been sick. Irene came in before he had finished.

"I've been out driving," she said, and sat down beside him at the dining-room table.

"With Boyd?"

"Yes. Did Ethel tell you?" Irene unbuttoned her left glove and then buttoned it again. "I've made up my mind, James—or rather I've had it made up for me. Boyd has to live in New York and I'd have to live there, too, it seems, if I went back to him."

"What are you going to do, then?"

"Stay here and help you look after the children."

From her expression it was impossible to tell whether the choice had been easy.

"Boyd is fonder of little Agnes than he is of me. I don't think he knows that, but he is. After he carried her off that time, I knew it. And I was afraid to have him see her. But I don't feel like that any more. He's so frightfully lonely. And there's no reason why he shouldn't have her part of the year. If I could be sure that I might be a different person, or that he could— but what has happened once can happen again. No matter what it is or how hard you try to avoid it. And where the going hasn't been too good it seems better not to double back on my own trail."

"No," James said, "I suppose not." But sooner or later she must do something. As it is, she has no life at all.

He put out his right hand and produced a chord —G, D flat, and F—on the dining-room table. Then he took a final drag at his cigarette.

"About the children, Irene—"

"It won't be easy, of course."

"I know that," he said.

"At first I wasn't at all sure that it could be done. Bunny was so close to his mother, you know. She seemed almost to be aware of every breath he took. And when they were in the same room together, he

was always turning his face toward her. Last night
when he came in and looked at me that way, I felt
that there was nothing that you or I or anyone else
could do for him. But this morning it's entirely different. The house is so bright, James, and so full of sunlight."

James leaned forward in his chair.

"I came in through the kitchen just now," Irene
said, "and when I saw Bunny making wreaths, I knew
somehow——"

Don't say it, James implored silently. *Don't say
it!*

"I knew that there was a chance that things might
work out all right. That we might be able to bring
them up in the way she would have wanted."

II

While the man from the undertaker's went back for
another load of chairs, there was time for James to
walk—to make the circuit from the library out into
the front hall, then through the living-room, which
was filled with flowers, and into the library again.

He would have preferred to walk alone, but Robert stood waiting at the foot of the stairs and James
did not have the heart to refuse him. Robert was freed
from his mistake. It was evident from the way he

walked. Neither Robert nor anyone else was responsible for Elizabeth's death. And anyway, it was what
people intended to do that counted—not what came
about because of anything they did. James saw that,
clearly. And he saw that his life was like all other
lives. It had the same function. And it differed from
them only in shape—as one salt-cellar is different from
another. Or one knife-blade. What happened to him
had happened before. And it would happen again,
more than once. Probably some one would lie awake
all night in that very same hospital feeling his lungs
contract and expand, contract, expand—until the
whole of him was limited to the one effort of breathing for somebody else . . . But it would not be Elizabeth who was dying of pneumonia two rooms down
the hall.

He would have liked to explain all this to Robert.
And about the rectangle of light on the ceiling above
his hospital bed. And also about the interurban,
which no longer bothered him. It would be years
probably before he could make Robert understand
what happened when he met Crazy Jake collecting
tin cans at midnight. But there was comfort at least in
Robert's company, and in resting his arm on Robert's
shoulders. Robert belonged to him. James could feel
that in the way they walked together. They were of
the same blood.

When he was Robert's age his father and mother
went South and took him with them, for the winter.
They rented a farmhouse on the side of a hill over-

looking a Confederate cemetery. And he had no one
to play with, being a Northerner, and he wanted to
go home.

James remembered that winter, though of all the
rest of his boyhood there was almost nothing left to
him. The remembrance of a cellar door that sloped
and could be used for hiding. A mulberry tree and
the smell of harness, and brown stain of walnuts on
his hands. . . . Even these things could not be shared
with Robert, who was growing up in a different
world.

Without their noticing it, they had changed the
direction of their walking, and it now brought them
straight toward the coffin. They stepped up to it, together, and it was not as James had expected. He did
not break down, with Robert beside him. He stood
looking at Elizabeth's hands, which were folded ir-
revocably about a bunch of purple violets. He had not
known that anything could be so white as they were
—and so intensely quiet now with the life, with the
identifying soul, gone out of them.

They would not have been that way, he felt, if
he had not been doing what she wanted him to do.
For it was Elizabeth who had determined the shape
that his life should take, from the very first moment
he saw her. And she had altered that shape daily by
the sound of her voice, and by her hair, and by her
eyes which were so large and dark. And by her wis-
dom and by her love.

"You won't forget your mother, will you, Robert?" he said. And with wonder clinging to him (for it had been a revelation: neither he nor anyone else had known that his life was going to be like this) he moved away from the coffin.

"Maxwell's voice is one of the wisest in American fiction; it is, as well, one of the kindest." —John Updike

ALL THE DAYS AND NIGHTS
The Collected Stories

The twenty-one stories in *All the Days and Nights* take us from a small town in turn-of-the-century Illinois to a precariously balanced enclave of the good life in Manhattan; together they make up what William Maxwell calls "a Natural History of home," a tour of the world that engages us entirely, and whose characters command our deepest loyalty and tenderness.

Fiction/Literature/0-679-76102-0

ANCESTORS
A Family History

Ancestors is the history of William Maxwell's family, which he retraces branch by branch across the wilderness, farms, and small towns of the nineteenth-century Midwest. Out of letters and journals, memory and speculation, Maxwell leads his readers into the lives of settlers, itinerant preachers, and small businessmen and makes us understand the way they saw their world and imagined the world to come.

Literature/Memoir/0-679-75929-8

THE CHÂTEAU

In 1948, two awestruck American tourists arrive at a stately château whose residents are just beginning to recover from the horrors and indignities of the war. Out of this tragicomic premise, William Maxwell creates the most astute and affectionate novel of cross-cultural incomprehension since the masterworks of Henry James.

Fiction/Literature/0-679-76156-X

THE FOLDED LEAF

This classic novel is the serenely observed yet deeply moving story of two boys finding one another in the Midwest of the 1920s. In his portrait of the lasting friendship between the two, William Maxwell reveals the impossibility of their longings and the keenness of their losses with an eye that is as forgiving as it is omniscient.

Fiction/Literature/0-679-77256-1

TIME WILL DARKEN IT

Time Will Darken It is a wryly funny and deeply compassionate novel of a small Midwestern town in the early years of the century. When Austin King befriends his young foster cousin, Nora, he unwittingly sets in motion a chain of events which could drastically alter every aspect of his life.

Fiction/Literature/0-679-77258-8